"*Virginia Kantra never ceases to amaze me.
All a Man Can Ask really packs a wallop,
combining h
heartwarming en
sexual tension. Alex is a potent and charming
hero, and Faye is a heroine you'll
for. A fabulously fun and delicio   d.
I loved it.*"

Her pulse went wild under his rough fingers.
Keeping his eyes on hers, he lowered his head,
blotting out the lake and the night behind her.
She felt the slow rise of heat, from him, in her.

And he stopped, a breath from her lips.

"I'm giving you a choice, Detective." Her mouth
curved. "Kiss me or die...."

Dear Reader,

A new year has begun, so why not celebrate with six exciting new titles from Silhouette Intimate Moments? *What a Man's Gotta Do* is the newest from Karen Templeton, reuniting the one-time good girl, now a single mom, with the former bad boy who always made her heart pound, even though he never once sent a smile her way. Until now.

Kylie Brant introduces THE TREMAINE TRADITION with *Alias Smith and Jones,* an exciting novel about two people hiding everything about themselves—except the way they feel about each other. There's still TROUBLE IN EDEN in Virginia Kantra's *All a Man Can Ask,* in which an undercover assignment leads (predictably) to danger and (*un*predictably) to love. By now you know that the WINGMEN WARRIORS flash means you're about to experience top-notch military romance, courtesy of Catherine Mann. *Under Siege,* a marriage-of-inconvenience tale, won't disappoint. Who wouldn't like *A Kiss in the Dark* from a handsome hero? So run—don't walk—to pick up the book of the same name by rising star Jenna Mills. Finally, enjoy the winter chill—and the cozy cuddling that drives it away—in *Northern Exposure,* by Debra Lee Brown, who sends her heroine to Alaska to find love.

And, of course, we'll be back next month with six more of the best and most exciting romances around, so be sure not to miss a single one.

Enjoy!

Leslie J. Wainger
Executive Senior Editor

Please address questions and book requests to:
Silhouette Reader Service
U.S.: 3010 Walden Ave., P.O. Box 1325, Buffalo, NY 14269
Canadian: P.O. Box 609, Fort Erie, Ont. L2A 5X3

All a Man Can Ask
VIRGINIA KANTRA

INTIMATE MOMENTS™

Published by Silhouette Books

America's Publisher of Contemporary Romance

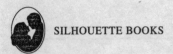

SILHOUETTE BOOKS

ISBN 0-373-27267-7

ALL A MAN CAN ASK

Visit Silhouette at www.eHarlequin.com

Printed in U.S.A.

Books by Virginia Kantra

Silhouette Intimate Moments

The Reforming of Matthew Dunn #894
The Passion of Patrick MacNeill #906
The Comeback of Con MacNeill #983
The Temptation of Sean MacNeill #1032
Mad Dog and Annie #1048
Born To Protect #1100
All a Man Can Do #1180
All a Man Can Ask #1197

*Trouble in Eden

VIRGINIA KANTRA

credits her enthusiasm for strong heroes and courageous heroines to a childhood spent devouring fairy tales. A three-time Romance Writers of America RITA® Award finalist, she has won numerous writing awards, including the Golden Heart, Maggie Award, Holt Medallion and *Romantic Times* W.I.S.H. Hero Award.

Virginia is married to her college sweetheart, a musician disguised as the owner of a coffeehouse. They live in Raleigh, North Carolina, with three teenagers, two cats, a dog and various blue-tailed lizards that live under the siding of their home. Her favorite thing to make for dinner? Reservations.

She loves to hear from readers. You can reach her at VirginiaKantra@aol.com or c/o Silhouette Books, 300 East 42nd Street, New York, NY 10017.

To Michael, with all my heart.

Special thanks to former police officer
and fellow writer Lynda Sandoval Cooper,
to Lieutenant Joseph T. FitzSimmons,
and to artist and friend Kristin Dill.

Chapter 1

He was back.

Faye Harper froze, her paintbrush poised over the wet paper. Heart thumping, she stared through the glass sliding doors toward the lake. The bright blue sky was wide and empty, the water dark and still. Soft greens and deep ochers defined the shore. The only signs of life were the dragonflies dueling in the air and the ducks squabbling around the weathered dock.

And the man in the navy windbreaker trespassing on her patchy strip of lawn.

Faye was almost sure it was the same man she'd spotted yesterday. And the day before. Dark-haired and broad-shouldered, too old to be a student and too neat to be a vagrant. But something about him—the set of his head or the tense line of his back or the coiled energy of that long, wiry body—pushed all her warning buttons and raised the fine hair on the back of her neck.

A blob of ultramarine dripped off her brush and onto

the wet paper. Faye hissed and grabbed a sponge to dab at the spreading blot. By the time she lifted the color and looked out her window again, the man was gone.

She inhaled slowly. Good. She'd fled to Eden to rest and to paint. She didn't need some tall, dark intruder disturbing her shaky peace.

Involuntarily she flexed her right wrist, testing for soreness. The fracture was healed. The cast had been cut off a week ago. But some hurts could not be bandaged over.

Seventeen-year-old Jamal's frustrated face flashed through her mind. *You can't help me. Can't nobody help me.* The memory tightened her chest.

She drew another deep breath. Jamal was right, she told herself. She had only made things worse. She knew better now.

She narrowed her focus to her painting, tipping the board so the colors flowed down the paper, lightly working water into the still-damp wash to turn the blot into a cloud. When she was almost satisfied, she glanced over at the sky.

And saw that man again, down by the dock.

Misgiving spread through her. She really, really did not want to get involved in confrontations. In explanations. But this was her aunt's land. This was Faye's vacation. She couldn't risk either one being ruined by the actions of a stranger.

What was he up to now?

She snatched her camera off the sofa table. Sidling to the glass doors, she fumbled with the zoom until she had the trespasser in her sights. He was prowling the muddy bank above the bushes with that long-legged stride she was beginning to recognize. She couldn't see his face. He was turned toward the lake, where a breeze broke the flat surface with shards of gold. She glanced across the water to the luxury homes on the far shore.

And then he pivoted toward the cottage, and she identified the glint of binoculars.

Okay. That was it. The final insult. The last straw.

Maybe Faye hated confrontation, but she wasn't standing around—literally—while some pervert peeped through her windows.

Her pulse racing, she set down the camera, picked up the phone and dialed 911.

It was a long time before the police came knocking at her door.

Faye hugged her elbows and paced Aunt Eileen's square living room, her wet-on-wet wash drying, her concentration wrecked. She thought she heard a car approach and went to the door.

Nothing.

But when she looked out her windows again, an officer with short hair and a cowlick was crossing the grass. Even with his outline thickened by whatever it was policemen wore under their clothes, he looked young and strong. Faye was reassured.

But her intruder wasn't frightened off. He stood with one leg slightly behind the other, his right arm down by his side, and waited for the young officer to come to him. Like a gunslinger, Faye thought.

They talked. Faye saw that, though she couldn't hear what they said. At one point, her trespasser reached for his hip pocket, and she held her breath. The last three years had made her suspicious of any gesture that could produce a knife or a gun. But he only pulled out—well, it was hard to tell, squinting through the camera lens—

but it looked like his wallet. He flipped it at the officer. They talked some more.

And then they started toward the house.

Her stomach sank. Oh, dear. She really didn't want...

The young officer bypassed the steps that led up to the deck. The two men disappeared along the side of the house. Maybe they would just go away?

Her doorbell rang. No.

Faye brushed her skirt with trembling fingers and went to open the door.

"Excuse me, ma'am." The young officer loomed on her porch. "Would you mind stepping out for a moment?"

Well, of course she minded. But she summoned her courage and a smile from somewhere and unlocked the screen door. Cautiously she edged out onto the porch. Her gaze slid sideways to her intruder.

Everything about him looked hard—hard face, hard body, hard, dark eyes. She shivered. She knew she made an unimpressive adversary, five-foot-two and twenty-five, with a little girl's short haircut and an old lady's flowered skirt.

Officer Cowlick cleared his throat. "I'm sorry to bother you, ma'am, but I have to ask. Do you know this man?"

She looked away, snapped from the hold of those bold dark eyes by a welcome jolt of outrage. "Is that what he told you?"

"He said that you'd seen each other."

Faye crossed her arms against her negligible chest. Indignation warmed her voice. "And I suppose if he told you those binoculars were for bird-watching, you'd believe that, too."

Her trespasser grinned.

The officer frowned. "No, ma'am. But I did check his ID. His driver's license lists him as Alec—Alex—"

"Aleksy," the intruder said.

"Denko," the officer snapped.

She was confused. "I don't know any Denkos."

"He does." Denko's voice was deep and confident. His eyes were wickedly amused. "Jarek Denko is the chief of police in this town."

She arched her eyebrows. "And who are you? His long lost cousin?"

He looked at her with a faint, surprised respect. "His brother."

She didn't want his respect. She wanted him gone. She appealed to the officer. "I don't care who his brother is. I want him off my property."

"Yes, ma'am. What I need to know is, will you be filing a formal complaint? Because—"

"Oh, dear God." She saw it now, as Denko swiveled to face the officer. A faint bulge at his back, covered by his jacket. "He has a gun."

The officer pivoted.

"Easy." Denko stepped back, palms up and wide. "It's in the belt clip at my back. I'll let you pat me down, but I don't want you getting excited and grabbing for the gun."

He turned around slowly, his hands still in the air. The officer leaned in and slid the gun from its holster before ducking away.

"Just a suggestion," Denko said over his shoulder. "Next time you might want to do the search before you bring a possible suspect up the complainant's porch steps."

The officer flushed dull red. "I'll have to detain you, sir. Please put your hands behind your back."

Faye's heart thumped with alarm.

But Denko only shrugged and held his wrists behind him. The officer snapped on the cuffs and tightened them.

Faye did not want to get involved. She really didn't. But some residual sense of responsibility forced her to ask, "Don't you have to, um, read him his rights or something?"

The officer slipped his fingertip out of the cuffs and took another step back. "He's not under arrest, ma'am."

"Then, why—"

"Only sworn law enforcement officers can carry concealed in Illinois," the officer said tightly.

"You've been watching too much TV, cream puff," Denko told her. "You don't have to Mirandize until you're going to question somebody. Usually at the station."

Faye goggled. *Cream puff?* What was with this guy? He was apprehended, disarmed and in handcuffs and yet somehow he wasn't subdued at all. A small part of her almost envied him.

The officer with the cowlick frowned. "Hey, are you on the—"

"At the station," Denko repeated. "I can fill you in there."

The two men exchanged glances. Faye felt more out of her depth than ever. "Yeah, okay," the officer said.

"Don't you need me to make a statement?" Faye asked.

The officer shifted his gaze to her. "We'll be in touch."

She watched him steer his prisoner toward the black-and-white cruiser. He'd parked on the side of the porch, under cover of Aunt Eileen's rhododendrons. Denko stood quietly while the officer opened the car door and put one hand on top of his head to guide him into the back seat.

Faye began to shake. *We'll be in touch.*

Apprehension formed a knot in her stomach. She could hardly wait.

"What the hell did you think you were doing?" Police chief Jarek Denko's voice was quiet and cold as a night in January. "This is my town. It's not your personal sandbox that you can come make a mess in when you're tired of stinking up Chicago."

Aleksy Denko clamped his jaw. He knew he was out of line, damn it. But he didn't allow anybody to talk to him that way. Not even his big brother.

"I was on a case," he said.

Jarek narrowed his eyes. "A case you didn't choose to explain to my patrol officer. A case you didn't bother to run by me. Damn it, Alex, you know the rules of jurisdiction."

"Yeah, well, I'm not exactly acting officially," Aleksy muttered. "I thought it was better if you didn't know."

"Let me get this straight. You kept me in the dark to protect me?"

Jarek sounded as if he couldn't believe it. Hell, Aleksy didn't believe it himself. Before his brother gave up the streets to play Andy Griffith in Eden, Jarek Denko—the Ice Man—had been a legend among the homicide cops of Chicago's Area 3.

"You want to tell me what this is all about?" Jarek invited quietly.

Aleksy sighed and dropped into the chair facing the

chief's desk. "You know about the shootout on the west side, five, six weeks ago?"

"I read about it in the paper. One officer down, I remember."

Aleksy remembered, too. He choked off the fresh wave of anger and guilt that rose with the memory. "Yeah, well, what wasn't in the paper was that it was a joint op. Some scum is running guns from Atlanta through Chicago to Canada. The Toronto police want him. The FBI wants him. The ATF wants him. And we got him. Set up a nice little sting to net the whole operation. Only everybody's tangoing so hard that somebody missteps. The scum figures it's a setup and gets away. We're left with nothing but a couple of mopes who aren't talking and one dead detective."

"How do you come into it? Was it your operation?"

"I don't like it when one of our own goes down. Maybe after the shooting, I pushed a little too hard on the investigation."

"No 'maybe' about it," Jarek murmured.

Aleksy grinned sharply. "Anyway, some fed got his toes stepped on and pushed back. Next thing I know, my boss is calling me into his office telling me I need an extended vacation."

"Here in Eden?" Jarek raised an eyebrow. "Not exactly Cancún, little brother."

"Could be I figured you needed some help planning your wedding."

A month or so back, Jarek had gotten himself engaged to a local babe. A reporter, Tess DeLucca. Aleksy had had some doubts about the match, but his brother seemed happy, and the wedding was set for September.

Jarek shook his head. "Which still doesn't explain

what you were doing on Eileen Harper's dock with binoculars and a gun.''

"The detective who was killed…" Aleksy hesitated and then shrugged. He had to give Jarek something, or he wouldn't get his gun back. "I knew her. Karen Vasquez.''

Jarek straightened behind his big metal desk. "Your partner?''

"Former partner," Aleksy corrected. "We stopped working together nine months ago. Before your move. Remember?''

"That's right. She put in for a transfer.''

"Yeah.''

"For personal reasons.''

Aleksy tried not to squirm. "Yeah.''

"How personal, hotshot?''

"Look, we were close. We got closer. Her idea, my mistake. Okay?''

"Not okay, if she couldn't work with you afterward," Jarek stated.

"I told you, it was a mistake. Anyway, she got reassigned. Coming from Area 3 she got handed this big case. Gunrunning across the border. She was excited. Called me up to tell me about it.''

"She shouldn't have done that.''

"She thought I might have an interest.''

"And what would that be? Aside from letting you know she was moving on to bigger and better things?''

"She said something about my brother finding himself in the middle of things. So when she—'' Died. Hell. "Anyway, afterward, I figured that was a lead up here.''

"But why—'' Jarek's eyes narrowed as he answered his own question. "Richard Freer. Liberty Guns and Ammo. His place is opposite the Harper dock.''

Aleksy nodded. "I tried to rent the cottage but the owner had already promised it to her niece."

The big-eyed pixie in the flowered skirt who had called the cops.

Jarek tapped a pencil against his desk. "Okay. I'll give you that Dick Freer is a pompous son of a bitch. But as far as I know, he's legit. And he's got a lot of pull in this community. Hell, he was on the search committee that hired me."

"Whoever our gunrunner is, he's got good cover. Or the feds would have caught him by now."

"And what makes you think you can succeed where they've failed?"

"I have to," Aleksy said.

Jarek's gaze sharpened. His voice softened. "It's not your job. It's not your case. You need to stay out of it."

"I can't."

"Alex—"

But Aleksy cut him off. He appreciated his brother's concern, but he didn't need it. He didn't want it. Some things were too painful to get into, and way too personal to share. "Are you going to stop me?"

His brother hesitated. "I can't let my department get mixed up in your personal vendetta."

"I know that. That's why I didn't spill the details to what's his name. Larsen. I just need you to leave me alone."

"That's it?"

"Well…you could give me my gun back."

Jarek opened a drawer in his desk and hefted Aleksy's snub-nose Smith and Wesson .38. "You carrying the 'chief's special' now?"

"You always did."

Jarek peered along the blue steel barrel. "Yeah, but yours is longer than mine."

"Barrel envy, big brother?"

Jarek's teeth glinted in a smile. "Yeah. What is yours, three inches?"

Aleksy laughed. "At least mine feels like a real gun instead of a kiddie toy."

Jarek raised his eyebrows, but he laid the gun flat on his desk without comment.

Aleksy slid it into the clip at his back. Some cops liked an ankle holster off duty, but he'd never been able to stand walking with one. "Thanks."

"You need a place to stay?"

Aleksy dropped his jacket over the gun to hide it. "No, I'm good. We're only an hour or so out of Chicago. I can get home occasionally to shower and change. Besides, the fewer people who associate you with me—or me with the police—the better."

"As long as you understand I expect to be apprised of your activity while you're in my jurisdiction."

Aleksy nodded to show he'd received the warning. "Understood."

"And, Alex...yell for help if you need it."

Aleksy grinned at his big brother. "Haven't I always?"

"Not always," Jarek said. "You let Tommy Dolan whip your butt in fifth grade."

Aleksy shrugged. "Fine. You want to help?" He did a mental playback of Faye Harper's wide eyes and unexpected spunk. "Fix things with the cream puff."

"—can only apologize and hope you're willing to forget about the matter," the police chief's cool, smooth voice said over the telephone line.

Faye's hand tightened on the receiver. He was talking down to her. A lot of people talked down to her. Too bad for the Denkos she was getting tired of it. "Most women would have difficulty forgetting an armed intruder."

The police chief coughed. "Actually, unless you previously communicated your desire for him to leave the property—if the yard were fenced, for example, or if signs were posted—he wouldn't be guilty of criminal trespass. Of course, I understand your—"

"He had a gun," Faye said.

The line was still for a moment. "A gun he was legally authorized to carry."

She knew it was futile to argue. But still. "Your officer said only sworn law enforcement officers could carry concealed firearms."

"Yes," the chief said, adding very gently, "My brother Alex is a detective with the Chicago PD."

The fight leaked out of Faye like air from a pricked balloon. What was the point of protesting? What was right was never as important as what was expedient. She should have learned that by now.

But the mocking memory of her trespasser's hard, dark eyes dared her to say, "And what was a detective from Chicago doing on my dock?"

Another pause. "I can't say."

"Can't, or won't?"

Jarek Denko was silent.

Don't get involved, Faye told herself. You don't want to know. She tucked the receiver under her jaw and used her left hand to massage her right wrist. Without the support of the cast, it ached when she used it too long.

"Never mind," she said. "I won't press charges or—

or whatever it is. I don't have time, anyway. I'm here to work.''

"Really?" the chief asked politely. Well, now that he had what he wanted—her cooperation—she supposed he felt compelled to be polite. "What kind of work do you do, Miss Harper?"

Once she would have told him with pride that she was a teacher. Now she stammered. "I, um…not work, exactly. I should have said I paint."

"Lots of pretty scenery up here," the chief said, still politely.

She made an agreeable noise—it seemed the fastest way to get him to leave her alone—and hoped he wouldn't start to tell her what views she ought to paint while she was here or about his aunt/sister/cousin who used to model clay/draw her own Christmas cards/do decoupage.

He didn't. He thanked her again formally and got off the line.

Faye drew a shaky breath and looked around her aunt's living room, now serving as her temporary studio. Brushes stood in mayonnaise jars. Paint dried in plastic trays. Photographs—a bright sailboat slicing the horizon, a flock of birds above an inlet, a skyscape at midday—spilled across the table. The metallic strip board she'd hauled from her Chicago apartment propped against one wall, her most recent work held in place with small round magnets.

I paint.

Beautiful scenes. Bright scenes. Safe scenes.

She bit her lip, aware of a faint dissatisfaction. Maybe they did lack a little of the energy and edge that characterized her earlier work, but they were pretty. Soothing.

Lame, Jamal would have said, with a shake of his head and his wide, white grin…

The tight control she'd held over her thoughts fissured, and through the gap, bitter self-accusation swept in a flood. Don't go there, she told herself. Do not. Go there. Don't.

She picked up one of the trays and headed to the kitchen to rinse out the old paints in the sink. She was scrubbing burnt umber from the palette's crevice when the doorbell rang.

Her heart began to thump. She turned off the water. She wasn't expecting visitors. She didn't know anyone in town, not really, and while she had left a forwarding address at the school, no one in Chicago cared where she'd gone. Mail delivery came around three and her aunt's cottage was too far off the beaten path to attract many salesmen.

Drying her hands on a paper towel, she went to the door. A man's tall outline blocked the afternoon sun. She squinted through the screen. Her misgiving swelled.

It was him.

Aleksy Denko.

Chapter 2

Aleksy was used to one of two reactions when he knocked on a woman's door. Either she stalled him while the man of the house bolted down the fire escape. Or, sooner or later, she invited him in for sex. Some women did both.

Faye Harper didn't look like she would do either one.

She hung back in the shadow of the house, her arms crossed and her body language shouting "go away." He didn't hold it against her. Even with Jarek's phone call smoothing the way, he probably made her nervous.

"It's okay," he said with an easy grin. He could do charming. Karen used to say it was his best interview technique, though he liked to think he had a nice line in subtly threatening, too. "I'm not selling anything."

Faye Harper didn't smile as he'd hoped and half expected. But she did take a half step closer to the screen. "That's good. Because I'm not buying. Anything."

This time his grin was for real. Score one for the

cream puff. And she looked cute, with her short blond hair and her small pale face, scowling at him through the screen. Cute wasn't his type, but he could understand the appeal.

"Well, now that we know where we stand, do you mind if I come in?"

She hesitated. "Will this take long?"

Not if she gave him what he wanted.

"I'll try not to take up too much of your time," he promised.

She unlocked the screen—he could have told her that was useless, any punk with a razor would cut through that flimsy barrier in seconds—and stepped aside to admit him. She smelled like spring flowers and line-dried sheets. He sniffed in appreciation.

She sniffed, too. "Can I see your ID?"

He gave her credit for asking and showed her his driver's license.

She studied it gravely and then asked, "Don't you have a badge?"

He winced. "A star," he said. "We call them stars. Security guards have badges."

The corners of her mouth dented, like she was amused, but she only said, "May I see it?"

He handed her the leather holder that held his detective's star with its black metallic band and raised white letters. He saw her surprise as its weight registered.

She turned it in her hand. "Why didn't you show this to the other officer this morning?"

She might be nervous, but she sure wasn't dumb.

"I didn't want to blow my cover," he said. "I'm working a case."

And if his lieutenant heard that one, he'd bust Aleksy's butt down to traffic patrol.

Faye tipped her head to one side. "Then why tell me now?"

He tried for a little sincerity. "Because I need your help."

"No."

Okay. Screw sincerity. Back to charm. "Maybe help is too strong a word," he said, leaning forward to take his star and her hand with it. "Cooperation."

She withdrew her hand, leaving the leather holder behind. "You'll have to recruit someone else. I'm not cooperating. Well, I'm not pressing charges, but that's as much as I can do. I can't afford to get involved. I'm here to rest and recover."

He looked her over. She looked good to him. "Been sick?"

She had very fine skin. She flushed. "Not really." But he noticed her left hand moved to cover her right wrist. Interesting.

"I'm on vacation," she said.

Not cooperating. And not divulging much, either.

"Faye—can I call you Faye?—what do you do?"

She moved her shoulders uncomfortably. "I teach."

That fit. He could see her in a kindergarten classroom, surrounded by adoring five-year-olds. She wasn't much more than a kid herself, with her wide brown eyes and her short, messy hair. Under that ridiculous skirt she wore, her narrow feet were bare. Unbelievably he got turned on looking at her feet.

Poor timing.

Remember Karen.

Do the job.

He switched his gaze back to her face. "A teacher, huh? Where do you teach?"

"Lincoln High School."

Lincoln? He almost whistled. The high school was adjacent to one of the most notorious projects in Chicago. Enrollment was high, graduation rates low, teacher burnout and turnover at epidemic rates. No wonder cream puff needed rest-and-recovery.

"What do you teach?" he asked, not just making conversation anymore.

"Art," she said flatly.

They must eat her alive.

He wouldn't mind a nibble himself.

But neither realization changed what he had to do.

Aleksy kept his voice low and his eyes level, inviting her trust. Implying a bond he was pretty sure she'd resist. "Well, then, I don't need to talk to you about doing your public duty. Teachers, cops, social workers…we're all on the same team."

"I'm sorry. It's been made painfully clear recently that I am not a team player."

He grinned. "Funny, my lieutenant says the same thing about me."

But Faye wasn't laughing.

"Look, I don't want to bother you," Aleksy said. "I just need your permission to hang around for a few days."

"A few days," she repeated.

"Yeah." Or a couple of weeks or however long it took to nail Karen's murderer.

"Why?"

"I've got to keep an eye on some things and your place is convenient."

"What kind of things?"

The hippie skirt and big lost eyes were deceptive. Under that flyaway blond hair, Faye Harper was sharp and stubborn. But when Aleksy was on a case, he was steel. He rubbed his jaw, pretending to consider. "I'm thinking the less I tell you about that, the less likely you are to be involved. You know?"

She frowned at having her own words turned back on her. "You promise I won't be involved?"

Aleksy smiled, satisfied he had her. "You won't even know I'm here," he promised.

He lied, Faye thought three days later as she readied her paper for painting.

She couldn't glance out her window or take out her trash without spotting Aleksy Denko ambling toward her woods or fishing from her dock. Even when he wasn't there, the possibility that he might appear hurried her heartbeat and diffused her focus.

She pulled a half sheet from the soaking tray, holding it by one corner to drain the excess water.

It wasn't that she was looking for him, she assured herself, giving the paper a gentle shake. Well, it wasn't *only* that she was looking for him. Tall, dark and in-your-face was tough to miss.

She placed the sheet on the drying board and smoothed it from the center to remove air pockets, taking comfort in the familiar gestures and the flat blank page. Her painting might be lacking these days, but her preparation was faultless.

Clackety clackety clackety clackety clack.

Faye started, nearly tearing a corner of the wet paper. What on earth—?

The racket continued outside her windows, close to the house. Metal on metal, *clackety clack.* Wiping her hands on her skirt, she edged to the sliding doors and peered out.

Aleksy Denko, stripped to the waist, paraded across

her strip of lawn, trundling her aunt's old push mower in front of him. The rusty blades made a terrible sound.

But it wasn't terror that dried Faye's mouth and quickened her pulse. It was the sight of all that gleaming, hot male flesh five yards away outside her window.

Close enough—her breath stuck in her chest—to touch.

He passed her. The lovely long lines of his back disappeared into the damp waistband of his jeans. She could see his buttocks flex. He leaned over the mower, head bent, shoulders taut, putting his back into the job the way he would work a woman.

He reached the end of the row and turned, revealing his sweaty, abstracted face and his deep, powerful chest with its shadow of hair. Not a boy. Not just a man. *All* man.

My goodness. Teaching high school hadn't prepared her for this.

His complete unawareness of her was both seductive and infuriating. He was a man mowing the lawn. Her lawn. And both the normalcy and the familiarity of the act pushed all her buttons.

It was intimate.

Unexpected.

Intolerable.

Ignoring the paper drying on the table, Faye rattled open the door and stepped out on the deck. "What do you think you're doing?"

Aleksy stopped. He looked up, his dark gaze colliding with hers. Something—desire? anticipation? dread?—fluttered in Faye's stomach.

He dragged his forearm over his sweaty face. "I'm mowing your grass."

"I can see that. I want to know why."

His full lips quirked in a smile. "Because it needs cutting?"

He was right. The lawn was disgracefully overgrown. And she'd meant to get around to it. Eventually.

"It's not your responsibility," she said, keeping her gaze on his face. Avoiding that hot, powerful chest.

He leaned on the mower handle. "So what? It makes your life easier. It makes my job easier, too."

"I don't understand."

"It's good cover. I'm less conspicuous mowing your grass than lurking around your house."

Her eyes flickered over his bare, broad shoulders, still winter pale, and his deep, muscled chest. He had a line of black hair, startling against his fair skin, that ran down his stomach and disappeared into… She jerked her focus back up.

"Not to me," she said crossly. "You're bothering me."

"Am I?" His tone was amused. Satisfied. Dangerous.

Her face burned. "The noise," she clarified. "The noise bothers me."

"Sorry." He didn't sound particularly sorry. "You want me to stop?"

Leaning against the rail above him, Faye caught the mingled scents of cut grass and hot male. She had another funny tummy flutter. "Well…"

"It's going to look bad if I quit now."

Faye surveyed the partially mown yard. He was right. "Well, I guess you could finish."

"Good." He grinned at her. "I hate to leave anything half-finished."

Her pulse pounded. That sounded like a warning. Or a dare.

Possibility expanded in her like orange pigment

spreading on wet paper. Three months ago, she might have taken up his challenge. Three months ago, she had a naive faith in herself and an inflated sense of her own ability to deal with things.

Faye stepped back from the deck rail, instinctively hugging her right arm against her chest. She couldn't deal with things anymore. She certainly couldn't handle whatever this hot, half-naked man was offering.

"I'll let you get back to it, then," she said, and reached behind her back to fumble with the sliding door.

His gaze sharpened. His smile faded. "Faye—"

"I have work to do." She turned tail and bolted like the coward she was.

It wasn't just cowardice, she told herself. She needed to get that sheet taped down before it dried or her morning's work would be wasted.

The pretty landscapes on the wall mocked her. Flat water. Empty sky. Her work was wasted anyway.

She pushed the thought away.

She cut the lengths of paper tape—*clackety clackety,* from the corner of her eye, she could see Aleksy, pushing, sweating—and pressed them to the edges of the drying sheet to stretch it—*clackety clack* as he passed the cottage again—and pinned the corners with thumbtacks.

Silence.

Faye straightened. Her back ached. Her heartbeat echoed in her ears. Was he gone?

Pressing a hand to the small of her back, she walked to the doors. The sun beat down on the green, empty strip of grass.

Gone.

She was…relieved. Of course she was relieved. She

refused to identify the sinking in her chest as disappointment. She turned back to her empty living room, but with all the quiet and time and space to create in she couldn't bring herself to pick up a paintbrush. Maybe she would go down to the lake and take photographs?

Yes. She nodded to herself. That would ease this odd restlessness. She stuffed her feet into sandals, grabbed her camera from the narrow table behind the sofa and went out the sliding doors.

Aleksy sluiced water over his arms. Standing waist deep in the cold lake might help cure his sexual frustration, but it didn't do a thing to relieve his itchy mood. After three days of surveillance, he had exactly nothing on Freer. No unexplained absences, no unknown visitors, no unauthorized stores of munitions in the gun dealer's boathouse.

Aleksy needed some action. Now.

A break in the case. A roll in the hay. Anything to kill the mind-numbing boredom and make this exile in Pleasantville feel like something besides a colossal waste of his time. Mowing pretty Faye Harper's lawn didn't count.

He thought of the tiny blonde's bare, arched feet, her wide, intrigued eyes and grinned. Now there was a woman who could provide a man with a little diversion.

Yeah, if he was dumb enough to let himself be distracted. Which Aleksy was not. Not yet. Not without some encouragement, anyway.

He dunked his head. And when he raised it dripping from the water, felt that unmistakable tingle at the back of his neck. His life preserver. The cop's sixth sense.

The awareness that someone, somewhere, was watching him.

Hell.

His sweat-soaked jeans were on the rocky bank behind him. His gun was out of reach, under his folded shirt. He'd better hope some vacationing tourist had stumbled on him skinny-dipping or he was in big trouble here.

He ran his hands over his face, like he needed to wipe the water from his eyes. He turned slowly, squinting through his fingers to scan the sloping bank.

The rocks were empty. His clothes were undisturbed. But a flash of pale blue—someone's shirt, he guessed— drew his attention up the bank. There in the bushes, a camera in her hands and pure confusion on her face, stood little Faye Harper.

Aleksy grinned. The day was looking up.

He lowered his hands. "Like what you see?"

Her fair skin made her an easy mark. She blushed bright red. "I didn't know you were here."

He believed her. But he couldn't resist teasing her. He shrugged. "Whatever."

"I didn't!"

He smiled.

She lifted her chin and some of the cream puff air fell away. "I don't think this arrangement is working. Frankly, Mr. Denko, you're intruding on my privacy."

He felt a moment's regret. But she couldn't get rid of him that easily. Not until he had proof one way or the other of Freer's complicity in Karen's death. "I'd go easy with the accusations, sweetheart. At least *I'm* not taking *your* picture in the buff."

"I was not taking your picture."

He gestured. "So, what's with the camera?"

She looked down at the camera in her hands as if she'd never seen one before. He stifled another grin.

"Oh. I'm taking backup shots of landscapes." Her voice gained confidence as she spoke. "To prompt my memory when I'm in the studio."

That was actually kind of interesting. Which just went to prove he'd been standing in the water too long.

"Yeah, well, you better turn your back," he said. "Or I'm going to give you something else to remember."

Her face set in cool, disapproving lines. He could almost see how Miss Pixie might have kept order in a classroom.

"That won't be necessary. I'm going into town now."

"Running away?"

"Running errands."

"That could be good," he decided. After five days of bug bites and boredom, he was ready for a new angle. Karen's lead only took him as far as the town. Maybe all this time, he'd been barking up the wrong tree. Staking out the wrong dock. "I'll come with you."

"No."

"It would be good cover," he said.

"I don't want you to come."

So she *was* running away. Aleksy tried to find that encouraging. Maybe he got to her the way she, improbably, got to him.

He observed her stiff face and the way she held her right arm braced across her chest. Or maybe she couldn't stand the sight of him.

"Just into town," he said. "You can let me out at— what is it?—Harbor Street."

Faye shook her head. "I'm sorry. I've let you stay,

but I won't be involved in—in whatever it is you're doing. You'll have to drive yourself to town.''

The unnaturally red-haired woman behind the counter at Weiglund's Camera—Greta, her name tag read— beamed at Faye as she popped her film into an envelope.

"You sure do take a lot of pictures for a single gal. Have you heard from your aunt Eileen yet?"

Faye blinked at the woman's intrusive interest. Friendly interest, she told herself. It couldn't hurt her. No one in Eden thought she'd done anything wrong. "I had a postcard from Galway. She thinks she's found the parish where her grandmother was born."

"Isn't that exciting," Greta Weiglund said, sealing the envelope and tossing it into a box behind her. "And do you like it at the cottage?"

"Yes, thank you."

"Not your first visit?"

"I— No. I used to come when I was a little girl."

"I thought I remembered that," Greta said with satisfaction. "Of course, you stayed with your auntie, then. Don't you find it lonely now?"

Dear heaven. "No. Are my other pictures ready?"

"Let me just check. I heard the police were out there the other day. A trespasser, was it?"

Faye fumbled with her wallet. Living in Chicago, she'd grown used to fending off muggers, purse snatchers and panhandlers. But she was defenseless against Eden's small town grapevine. "It wasn't anything. A— a misunderstanding."

Greta twinkled knowingly. "A young man, I heard. Are you seeing each other?"

Faye had a mental flash of Aleksy half-naked in the

lake, the damp hair curling on his chest, his dusky nipples puckered with cold. *Seeing* each other?

"I— That is—"

I didn't want to blow my cover, he'd told her. *I'm working a case.*

Faye bit her lip. "I guess you could say we see each other occasionally."

Greta Weiglund nodded encouragement. "Isn't that nice?"

It was awful.

Faye did not want to get involved. On her way back to the car, past the Rose Farms Café and Tompkins Hardware, she rehearsed to herself all the other things she could have said to deflect gossip.

I'm not sure who you're talking about.

We're just friends.

That's Raoul. He does the yard work.

"Faye!"

A man's voice. Calling her name. She froze. But it was only Richard Freer smiling at her from the gleaming glass entrance of his sporting goods store, as well-groomed and ruggedly handsome as a race car driver hawking motor oil.

Eileen Harper didn't like him. "Cuckoos," she called him and the other wealthy residents who bought up land across the lake to build newer, grander houses. But he was the closest thing to a neighbor Faye had. They seldom spoke, but he always waved when he saw her.

He strolled forward onto the sidewalk. "I know Eden's not the big city, but I didn't know you were so hard up for entertainment here that you'd started talking to yourself."

She forced a smile. "Hi, Richard. Sorry. I was distracted."

"I could see that." He looked her over with the confident air of a man used to paying for—and getting—what he wanted. Faye caught herself stiffening and ordered her muscles to relax. He didn't mean anything by it. And she'd given up taking stands over things she couldn't control.

"I haven't seen you on the lake," he said. "What are you doing with yourself?"

She wondered if she should try out her yard boy explanation on him. *No.* "Nothing much."

His gaze focused on the bag she carried. "Still taking pictures?"

They were neighbors, of sorts. He'd seen her out with her camera, and she'd explained about her painting.

"A few."

"Heard you had some trouble at your place the other day." He shifted closer and lowered his voice. "You know, a woman alone should always have protection at hand."

He couldn't mean… Condoms?

"No, ma'am, you don't want to be caught unprepared if a situation arises suddenly where you need it."

Faye goggled.

"A gun," Richard said firmly. "A nice, light ladies' handgun, that's what you need."

"Oh." Faye's breath escaped on a shaky laugh. "I don't think—"

"You've got to take care of yourself. A couple of vagrants have been spotted at the lake. I've seen one myself, hanging around your aunt's cottage."

Her relief died. "Well, actually—"

"Hi, sweetheart." Aleksy's warm, rough voice broke

into her explanation. His warm, heavy arm wrapped around her shoulders. "Sorry to keep you waiting."

And before she could get her mind or her tongue working, before she could react or protest or prepare, he bent his dark head and kissed her full on the mouth.

Chapter 3

He tasted like coffee.

He needed a shave.

And he had absolutely no business putting his tongue anywhere near her lips.

Faye registered all this in the brief, confused moments when Aleksy's hard arm squeezed her shoulders and his mouth crushed hers. Wild heat bloomed in her chest and in her face. Indignation, she told herself. Had to be.

And then Aleksy released her and turned his careless, all-guys-together grin on Richard Freer.

"I don't think we've met," he said. "I'm Alex."

"Dick Freer."

They shook in a ritual less complicated but no less appraising than the high fives and hand signals of Lincoln High's homeboys.

"Are you in town long?" Richard asked.

"As long as Faye will have me," Aleksy said. *And*

don't you forget it, she thought, her lips still tingling from his kiss. "You?"

"I'm lucky enough to live here." Richard straightened proudly against the plate-glass entrance. "This is my shop."

"Guess you don't get to travel a lot, then."

Richard pulled in his jaw, creating an important-looking double chin. "Oh, I get around. Trade shows. Gun shows."

Aleksy nodded. "Ever get down to Chicago?"

"Not often. Most of my business is selling shotguns and rifles to local sportsmen. And self-defense, of course."

"What kind of self-defense are we talking about?"

"Whatever makes a man feel free and his family safe. Are you interested in guns, Alex?"

Faye wriggled out from under Aleksy's arm. He was too close. This was too weird. And she wasn't crazy about Dick Freer's aggressive salesmanship, either.

Aleksy let her slide from under his elbow and then caught her fingers in his. "I could be," he said.

Richard's smile broadened. "Are you a gun owner?"

"Well, no. Not yet."

Faye frowned. He was lying. Why was he lying? "We really need to go now." Aleksy gave her a sharp look. She bit her lip. "Dear."

He shrugged. "Okay, babe. Nice talking with you," he said to Richard Freer.

"Come back and see me," the dealer invited.

"Count on it," Aleksy said.

Faye breathed a sigh of relief as they started down the sidewalk toward the tiny municipal parking lot. She caught a glimpse of their reflections in the window of the Silver Thimble—short, blond and flustered, barely keeping pace with tall, dark and annoyed—and was amazed that she'd stood up to him. But everything was all right now. In another minute she'd be in her car and going home. Alone.

"Do you mind telling me what the hell you were running away from back there?"

Indignation rendered her almost speechless. Almost. "Excuse me?"

"I wanted to talk with that guy."

She dug in her canvas bag for her keys. "Why?"

"You don't want to know."

"Exactly." Her keys jangled in the bottom of the bag. "I *don't* want to know. I can't afford to get mixed up in whatever it is you're doing." Her hand closed on her keys but Aleksy was in her way, leaning against her door, arms folded indolently over his chest in this sort of macho slouch. Her pulse speeded up.

"I don't want you kissing me, either," she said.

"Fine."

She searched his eyes. "I mean it."

"Don't worry about it. You're not my type."

She raised her chin. "Really."

"Yeah." He grinned crookedly. "So you can relax."

"I am relaxed. Or I will be, as soon as you leave."

He jerked his head toward the broken line of cars. "I'm parked here."

She looked. He drove a TransAm: low-slung, high-geared, dark and dangerous looking. Unsafe at any speed, she thought, and shivered.

"Then you won't need a ride," she said.

He uncrossed his arms. "Careful, cream puff. You might hurt my feelings."

"I'm not worried. I'm not your type, remember?"

"No, but you are tasty."

Three months ago she would have known how to answer him. She was still searching for a response when he pushed off from her car and strolled over to his.

"See you at home," he called. The TransAm started with a testosterone-spewing roar.

Faye yanked on her car door. "Not if I see you first," she muttered.

Which wasn't at all the kind of I'm-in-charge-class comeback she was looking for, but she was out of practice.

Faye stepped back and surveyed her morning's effort. She had hoped maybe this time she had something special: a moody blend of light and dark, a study in atmosphere. Her photos spread sharp and bright across the table. Her open sketchbook captured the creamy hull and coral sky reflected in the shifting surface of the lake at dawn. But when she looked at her painting, she saw only a flattened boat on overworked water. Murky. Muddy. Muddled.

Crud.

It wouldn't even make good sofa art.

Let your work express your feelings, she used to lecture her students. The gnawing dissatisfaction of the past few months developed new teeth. Maybe her feelings were the problem. Maybe instead of letting herself be stalled by her painting and stumped by Detective You-Don't-Want-to-Know Denko and just generally frustrated, she should pick up the phone and check on Jamal.

Faye winced and rubbed her wrist. She'd been holding a brush too long.

Or maybe she'd simply had it with this particular piece of work.

She needed...inspiration. She stretched once to get the kinks out, slapped shut her sketchbook and shoved it into her bag. She would take a walk down by the lake and clear her head.

"You know, for an artist, you don't seem to spend a lot of time painting," Aleksy said.

Below him on the bank, knee deep in the green brush, Faye Harper froze like Bambi's mother about to get shot. Her head turned slowly.

And then she spotted him, propped against a tree trunk with his fishing pole and field pack. Her wide brown eyes narrowed in annoyance. "For a detective, you don't seem to spend a lot of time investigating."

Ouch. Bambi's mom was packing heat.

Despite his frustration, Aleksy grinned. "I hit a snag."

She picked her way over roots and rocks toward him. "Fish not biting?"

"I didn't expect them to. No self-respecting striper's going to feed in the middle of the day."

"Then what are you doing out here?"

"Surveillance," he said briefly.

"What are you looking for?"

He shook his head. "You don't—"

"—want to know," she finished for him. "Thank you. Is it safe for me to sit down next to you?"

His grin broadened. "Be my guest."

Her skirt billowed and collapsed around her. She wore sandals on her narrow feet and a scoop-necked T-shirt that revealed the slight upper slope of her chest. Her face was pink and moist and she smelled like heat and spring flowers.

Tasty, he thought.

But not on the menu. He wasn't on vacation, whatever his lieutenant said. And a cream puff art teacher with baby-fine skin didn't fit into his plans or his future.

"Did you want something?" he asked.

"Yes. No." She rested her arms on her knees and her neckline gaped, revealing the white line of her bra. Oh, man. He had definitely been sleeping in his car too long, if a glimpse of ladies' underwear made him hard.

"I hit a snag, too," she said.

"What kind of snag?"

"You wouldn't understand."

Probably not. He didn't know squat about painting. But her automatic dismissal rankled.

"Try me," he said, surprising them both.

He didn't *do* intimacy. No way was he discussing art with a woman he wasn't even trying to talk into bed.

"I'm not—I seem to be putting in a lot of effort without a lot of result," Faye said.

Well, hey, okay. "I can relate there."

She turned her head and looked at him. "Have you found…whatever it is you're looking for yet?"

"Nope."

"But you're going to keep looking," she guessed.

"Yep."

"Why?"

Because he owed it to Karen. He owed it to himself.

"That's my job," he said.

"Shouldn't you have help? I don't know, but—a partner or something?"

His former partner was dead. Murdered. His current partner, Kenny Stivak, thought he ought to let the big boys handle the case. And Aleksy's boss told him if he didn't back off, he'd be busted down to directing Sunday traffic in the St. Wenceslaus parking lot.

"I don't need help," he said.

She sniffed. "That's what my students say. Usually the ones who are most in danger of quitting. Or failing."

"Well, I'm not going to quit and I can't afford to fail, so you can save the lecture. Teacher."

She flushed. She really had the damnedest skin, as fine and delicate as one of the teacups in his mother's china cabinet. "I haven't actually decided whether I'll return to teaching next year."

Now there was a surprise. "At Lincoln?"

She took a deep breath. "At all."

Against his will, he felt the drag of interest. It wasn't just that she was cute and he was bored. Faye Harper had...something, he decided. Smarts, maybe. Or guts.

Which made her comment about leaving teaching puzzling.

"How come?" he asked, figuring she'd say something about teacher burnout or the lousy pay or the school board cutting arts funding again.

"The principal and I didn't see eye to eye on my handling of a student."

"Parents?" Sometimes it helped in juvenile cases to get a kid's family involved. Although, at Lincoln, where families struggled simply to survive, lots of parents no longer had the energy to care.

"The mother wouldn't speak with me. The stepfather was more...forceful in his opinions."

"He disagreed with you."

Faye stared out over the water. "He broke my wrist."

Aleksy was startled into bobbling his line. He made a grab for the pole. She was a tiny thing. No threat to anyone. What kind of man would raise a hand to her? Anger burned his gut. "You press charges?"

"No. It was an accident," she explained. "He was trying to make me leave the apartment, and I—fell—down the stairs."

"He pushed you, you mean. That's aggravated assault."

"It was an accident. At least…" Her left hand moved unconsciously to cover the wrist on her knee. The gesture made sense now. "The principal advised me it would be better to treat the incident as an accident."

"Better for who?"

"For Jamal. My student."

Aleksy was disgusted. "The one who caused the problem in the first place."

She shook her head. "No. No, Jamal was never a problem. He was an excellent student."

"Then, why—"

"He was an excellent student," she repeated. "Talented in math. Brilliant in art. I pulled every string I had to get him accepted as a scholarship student at the Art Institute school."

"So, what was the trouble?"

"Jamal's parents—his stepfather—wanted him to go to a regular college and get a degree in business."

Aleksy shrugged. "Sounds reasonable to me."

"Yes. It sounded reasonable to everyone," Faye said bleakly. "And heaven help Jamal if what was reasonable in this case wasn't right for him."

"So, what did you do?"

"It doesn't matter now."

It mattered, he thought. To her, if to no one else. Even if she hadn't confessed she might ditch her job, he could see for himself the stress that haunted her eyes and compressed her mouth.

"Come on. What did you do?"

She stood, close enough that her skirt brushed his arm. His body reacted to her warmth and the scent that fell from her skirt. He hardly had to move his hand and he'd be touching her smooth calf, her warm thigh. He grinned a little at his own fantasy. He could reach right under all that flowery material and—

"I learned I had no business butting in where I wasn't welcome," Faye said.

Aleksy's grin sharpened. She might feel down, but she definitely wasn't out. "With that kind of attitude, you'd make a lousy cop."

Her eyes met his, direct and sad, and his amusement cut off like a spigot.

"I made a very bad teacher," she said. "Excuse me."

He watched as she scrambled down the bank and back toward the cottage. Her pale legs flashed along the water's edge.

He was losing his objectivity, damn it. She was just a convenience. And he was a cop. It was time he started thinking like one.

In his experience, only the very innocent and the very guilty ran from questioning. He wondered if anyone could be as innocent as Faye Harper seemed.

Or what she had to hide.

She was running away. Again. And it was beginning to tick her off.

Faye's sandals slipped on shale and stone. She didn't used to be such a loser.

She could have kept her mouth shut. She grabbed at a sapling for balance. Instead she'd let herself be lured by Aleksy's hot dark eyes and easy grin. She'd allowed herself to be seduced by the promise of his understanding. She'd opened her big fat mouth and fallen in, and it wasn't even his fault. Her hand came away sticky and smelling of tar.

Sure it was.

He was a detective. He probably knew all kinds of ways to get people—to get women—to talk to him. And she had. All it had taken were a few quick questions and a brief show of indignation, and she was right back where she didn't want to be, revisiting a topic she'd promised herself was over and done with.

With relief, she saw her aunt's cottage up ahead. Its weathered gray shingles and shabby trim shone in the sun. Ducks dozed in the shadow of the dock. All quiet. Peaceful. And hers, at least for the next few months.

Only now its peace had been disturbed. By Alex Denko.

She could have excused him for polluting the atmosphere with high level pheromones.

She couldn't blame him for listening when she'd been willing to talk. Faye frowned. *Anxious* to talk.

But she could not forgive him for forcing her to see that, deep down, she still cared desperately about her job. About Jamal. And she must not care. Her health and her sanity depended on it.

She climbed the steps to the deck, one hand already digging in her bag for her keys. Sunglasses, sketchbook, wallet… There they were. She pulled them out and froze with the keys clutched in her hand.

The door was already open.

Not all the way, which explained why she hadn't noticed it before. But there was a two-inch crack between the sliding panel and the aluminum frame, where she was sure—almost sure—she had pulled the door shut and locked it behind her.

Which meant... Which meant... Oh, dear. Her stomach hollowed.

Heart pounding, she took a deep breath, as if she could force oxygen to her brain to get it working. This wasn't Chicago, she reminded herself. She wasn't going to be assaulted in her aunt Eileen's living room by some twitchy kid or strung out junkie desperate enough to follow her home.

But her door was undeniably open.

She peered through the dark glass at the shadowed interior. And there was no way she was going inside alone.

Slowly, she backed down the steps. When she felt the soft ground under her feet, she turned and started to run.

She didn't have far to go.

The noise of her panicked passage must have traveled ahead of her. Faye was barely under the cover of trees when she saw Aleksy Denko prowling through the brush like a K-9 dog on high alert, head high, face grim. Despite the pole he still carried, no one in their right mind would mistake him for a casual middle-of-the-week fisherman.

She almost sank with relief. She waved instead.

He strode toward her and caught her elbows in both hands, steadying and supporting her. "You all right?"

"Yes. I'm—" *spooked* "—fine."

His expression didn't change. "What happened?"

"I don't know. I got back to the cottage and—" She swallowed. Was she overreacting? "Well, the door was open."

"Did you lock it? When you left?"

"I think so."

"Did you go inside?"

She felt like an idiot. "No."

"Smart girl. Stay here." He dropped her arms and loped away.

"Hey!" she yelled weakly. "Shouldn't you call your brother?"

He ignored her. Or maybe he didn't hear. Or maybe he figured he was saving her embarrassment, not calling in Officer Cowlick when there was nothing wrong except she was a neurotic nuisance who hadn't latched her door properly.

But she had. She was almost sure of it.

Aleksy reached the tree line. Beyond him she could see a patch of sunlit grass and her aunt's gray cottage. He slid out of his pack, laid down his fishing pole and pulled his gun from the small of his back.

Her breath caught in her chest. Oh, dear God.

She hurried forward. At the edge of the trees, she stopped. *Stay here,* he had ordered, and she didn't have any better ideas.

It was like watching a movie, she thought. Aleksy disappeared along the side of the house, moving fast and low. Faye waited, her stomach churning, until she saw him come round the opposite corner.

He sort of flowed up the steps to the wooden deck and flattened himself against the wall, out of sight of anyone who might still be inside. He knocked on the weathered shingles.

"Police!"

No response. At least, none that Faye could hear.

He repeated the knock. "Police!"

He shoved the door back along its track and vanished inside. Faye waited with her heart in her throat and her hands pressed to her mouth. A minute crawled by. Two minutes.

Aleksy strolled out onto the deck. "You want to come tell me if you think anything's missing?" he called.

She started to breathe again. She could do that, she thought, crossing the grass. Unless the thief had rifled through her aunt's drawers…

She looked up into Aleksy's expressionless face. "Is it bad?"

He jerked his head toward the open door. "See for yourself."

She stepped over the aluminum threshold, giving her eyes a moment to adjust to the change in light. She frowned in confusion.

Not bad at all. In fact—

"You still got your TV and VCR." Aleksy's voice behind her made her jump. "So your intruder wasn't interested in fencing electronics. You might want to check your bedroom for jewelry."

She hurried down the short, dark hallway, very aware of him stalking her. Her room looked the way she had left it, the comforter pulled up carelessly over the bright print sheets, her bottles and lotions arranged haphazardly on the dresser, her underwear spilling out of a drawer…

She flushed and scooped a pair of panties off the floor. "Sorry it's such a mess."

Aleksy propped his shoulder against the door. "Was it a mess when you left this morning?"

"Yes," she confessed.

He smiled. "Anything missing?"

"I—" She did a quick survey of her dressertop, jerked open the drawer that held her jewelry. She stared at the tangle of silver chains and colored stones and dangly earrings, all of it pretty and none of it very valuable. "I don't think so."

"Too bad."

"Excuse me?"

"I'd feel better if you got ripped off."

She stiffened with outrage and embarrassment. "I'm sorry if you feel I wasted your time."

His mouth compressed. "You didn't waste my time, cream puff. You definitely had an intruder. I looked at your frame. The door was forced. But if you didn't get robbed, we have to assume whoever broke in was looking for something."

"Like what?"

He shrugged. "Like me. Maybe somebody was checking for ID."

She did not want to be involved. "Why would someone do that?"

"Could be somebody around here isn't comfortable with strangers. Could be they made me as a cop."

"That would explain why you were on my deck with your gun drawn shouting, 'Police,'" she said dryly.

Chagrin drew his brows together. "Yeah, well, let's hope they missed that. Your bad guys were probably off the premises by then."

"I still don't understand why they would search my cottage if they were looking for you."

"They might have hoped to find my star or my gun. But I'm carrying those. Or they could've been after some sign that I'm really living here with you."

"But you're not," she protested.

His eyes met hers, dark and direct. "Then we've got a problem, don't we?"

Chapter 4

She was not going to panic.

He couldn't make her do anything she didn't want to do. Faye met Aleksy's hard, implacable gaze. Her stomach flopped. Could he?

In her best teacher voice, she said, "I'd feel more comfortable if we continued this discussion somewhere other than my bedroom."

He grinned, and her stomach flip-flopped again. "Whatever you want, sweetheart."

"What I *want* is for this whole situation to go away," she said. "But that's not going to happen, is it?"

He looked briefly regretful. "Probably not," he admitted.

Even though she was expecting his answer, it came as a blow. She tried not to flinch. "Okay." She tugged the door shut behind him and led the way back to her living room studio, trying to get control of herself and the situation. "Then the more pertinent question is, what do I have to do?"

"Call the police."

She stopped. "You're police."

"This isn't my jurisdiction."

"But if nothing's been stolen—"

"You should still call it in. You notify the local police department, they can beef up patrols, file a report, maybe dust for fingerprints."

"That's what you want, isn't it?" The realization sharpened her voice. "You want to find out who was here without it looking like you're the one who wants to know."

He didn't deny it.

She felt slightly sick. Used. "You said I wouldn't be involved."

"You're already involved."

"Because someone thought you were living here," she insisted. "Now they know you're not."

He raised his eyebrows. "If they know that, then they have to think you were lying. And they're going to wonder why."

She stared at him, her stomach churning.

"Call the police," he said again, his voice gentle. "See what the chief says."

She remembered the smooth voice over the phone. "He's your brother. He'll say whatever you want him to."

Aleksy shook his head. "Jarek's one of the good guys. He'll do whatever he thinks he has to to protect you."

Police chief Jarek Denko was like his voice, polite, controlled and serious. He arrived within ten minutes of

Faye's call. A female officer, lean and graceful as a greyhound on a leash, stalked beside him. Aleksy went down the steps to meet them.

Faye watched from the porch as they communicated in terse phrases and unspoken signals, as foreign to her as if they really were the animals they resembled. *Sniff, sniff, wag, wag, growl.* A bubble of amusement rose in her throat.

And then they turned in a pack to face her and she swallowed hard.

"Miss Harper?" The chief of police was a more compact version of his brother, equally intense and almost ten years older. Aleksy's eyes were dark as coffee. Jarek's were light as frost. "I'm Jarek Denko. We spoke on the phone."

It was stupid to feel breathless. "Yes, I—I know."

He smiled Aleksy's smile, with more understanding and less edge. She wasn't reassured, but she caught herself smiling back. "Do you mind if we sit down?"

"Oh. No. Please." She retreated to the living room and dropped into a chair, clasping her hands tightly in her lap.

The chief sat forward on Aunt Eileen's comfortable, ugly couch, his notebook balanced on his knee. Aleksy propped against the fireplace, his hands in his pockets and his eyes on her face.

Faye straightened her spine. Ridiculous to feel as if she were a troublemaker called to the principal's office. But she did.

She hadn't done anything *wrong,* she reminded herself. But it didn't matter. She hadn't been wrong to recommend Jamal for an art scholarship, either, and she'd still had to face a reprimand from the principal.

"Just a few routine questions," Jarek said. "Baker, why don't you see what that door will tell us."

The young female officer sprang to the sliding doors and pulled out a flashlight. Faye watched as she angled the beam one way and another.

"Latents?" Aleksy asked.

Officer Baker, her long, dark hair pulled back smoothly from her narrow face, looked to her chief, clearly waiting for his command.

"Dust it," Jarek ordered. "Now, Miss Harper…"

Faye did her best to answer his questions, trying to ignore the young woman shaking fine black powder off a fat black brush all over her aunt's door frame, and Aleksy, alive and restless by the fireplace.

"And that's when you went to find Alex?" Jarek prompted.

"Yes," Faye said. "I was—just a little nervous."

Not nervous, she thought miserably. Cowardly.

"Not nervous," Aleksy corrected her. "Smart."

Jarek turned his head and regarded his brother. "And what were you doing on Miss Harper's property?"

"Fishing."

"Do you have a license?"

Aleksy straightened away from the mantel. "What?"

"A license," Jarek repeated, deadpan. "To fish."

"Bite me," Aleksy said.

Jarek raised an eyebrow. "Get one."

"Jare, you know I'm not after—" He looked at Baker and stopped.

"As long as you're here, you'll do everything by the book," Jarek said. "Everything. You got me?"

They would make an interesting study, Faye thought. Two brothers stamped with the same harsh Slavic cheekbones and passionate Slavic mouths. One all hot energy, one all cool control. In her mind, she began to draw them.

"I'll see what I can do," Aleksy said.

"That's what worries me," Jarek murmured.

Aleksy grinned. "Can you run the prints?"

Jarek looked at Baker. The young woman shook her head. "No prints," Jarek said. "Sorry, Miss Harper. We'll keep an eye out, but unless they try again, it's unlikely we'll know who broke in."

He spoke to her. But Faye thought his words were meant for Aleksy.

"I understand," she said. "Thank you for coming."

Jarek stood, tucking his notebook away. "Anytime. Don't let this spoil your vacation. You have a nice place here."

"It's my aunt's," she said, compelled to qualify. To apologize. To explain, following the pattern she'd been forced into since her disastrous error of judgment three miserable months ago. "I'm only borrowing it for the summer."

"I know. To paint, you said." He gestured to the sheets of paper tacked to the display board and stacked on the table. "This your work?"

She felt compelled to apologize for that, too. "In progress."

Aleksy strolled over from his post by the fireplace. "What are you working on now?"

"That wet-in-wet of the boat at dawn. It's not very good yet."

"What's a—" He stopped himself. "Show me."

Impatiently she stepped to the table. "I only started it this morn—" She broke off.

Aleksy's eyes narrowed. "What?"

Dumbfounded, she stared at the blank spot in the center of her work space. "It's gone."

Jarek withdrew the notebook from his breast pocket. "Your painting?"

Aleksy's sharp gaze swept the table. "What else is missing?"

"Nothing. That is— The photographs," she said uncertainly. "I had an entire roll developed yesterday. Right here."

The two brothers exchanged glances.

"Bingo," said Aleksy.

"Do you remember the subject of the photographs, Miss Harper?" Jarek asked.

She ran a hand through her hair. "Not really. I didn't take any one subject," she explained. "I like to get different images on film. I do field sketches, of course, but you can get so much more detail with photographs. Rocks, water, interesting vegetation…"

Aleksy scowled. "But the missing painting—that's of a boat, right?"

"Yes."

"Do you know whose boat? Where was it?"

His investigation was spilling and flowing into her life like a watercolor wash gone horribly wrong. Her home had been invaded. Her work had been stolen. And from Aleksy's rising excitement, she sensed things were about to get even worse.

"It was tied up across the lake."

"At Freer's dock? Is it his boat?"

Oh, dear. "I don't think so. That is, I only saw it there once. When I went back the next morning, it was gone."

By the doors, the uniformed officer was quietly packing her bag to go.

"What type of boat?" Jarek asked.

She spread her hands in frustration. "A *boat* boat. Not a sailboat. I don't know boats. It was sort of beige."

"Beige." Aleksy blew out a short, exasperated breath. "I thought artists were supposed to be observant."

"Ask me about the quality of light or the contrasts in tone," she flashed back. "For everything else, I've got snapshots."

He grinned, his good humor apparently restored by her own display of artistic temper. "And did you take a snapshot of the boat?"

She elevated her chin. "I took several."

"All of them missing?"

She pushed at a stack of half-finished paintings; lifted a plastic palette. "Yes. The whole roll is gone."

"Could you have misplaced them?"

She was too used to questioning her own judgment to resent his question. Much. This was her work they were talking about. "No. They were on this table this morning. I'm sure of it."

Jarek scratched at his jaw with the end of his pen. "Who knows about your picture-taking habit, Miss Harper?"

Her uncertainty returned. "I suppose anyone could have seen me out with the camera... And I get the film developed in town."

"Weiglund's Camera?"

She supposed in a small town the chief of police would know most of the merchants. But it was oddly charming, all the same. "Yes."

"Well, if Greta Weiglund knows about you, then everybody in town knows," Jarek said, with a glint of humor that was hard to resist. "Thanks, Laura. That'll be it."

Officer Baker let herself out the front door.

"Faye." Aleksy leaned in on her other side with the steady look and oh-so-sincere smile he'd tried on at their first meeting. She was flanked by Denkos. Surrounded. "It would really help us out if you could describe the boat."

She was not amused. She would not be charmed. But she might be helpful, and, if she were lucky, they would go away.

"I can do better than that," she said. "I can show it to you."

Excitement flared in his eyes. "Where? How?"

Oh, my. She smoothed her hands down her skirt, trying to hide their trembling. "The photos are only backups for the sketches. I still have my sketchbook."

His smile warmed to something real. "Clever girl," he said softly. "Show me."

She flushed and dug in her canvas bag for her pad. She thumbed through the watercolor sketches—color impressions of a cloud-layered sky, a wooded bank, posts in a river with the sun behind them—until she found her study of a moored boat at dawn.

Both men bent over the table to look.

"Do you recognize it?" Jarek asked Aleksy.

Aleksy grunted. "Not from my files. You?"

"It's a beige boat with a cabin."

"You're a fat lot of help."

Jarek smiled thinly. "You want me to take it further?"

"Take what further?" Faye demanded and then bit her lip. She didn't want to know. She didn't want to be involved.

The Denkos ignored her anyway.

"I'll take it. For now," Aleksy said.

"Don't step on any more toes," his brother warned. "I've got a good relationship with the feds and I want to keep it that way."

"Don't worry. I'm unofficial."

"Be very unofficial," Jarek said. "Start with Mark."

Aleksy looked revolted. "DeLucca?"

"He knows boats."

"Yeah, but—"

"He's going to be family."

"Ain't that a kick in the head," Aleksy muttered.

Jarek pinned him with a look. Faye's fingertips tingled at the sudden tension in the room.

Aleksy sighed. "Okay. I'll talk with him. Tonight."

Jarek nodded. His gaze, cool as lake water, met Faye's. "Miss Harper. I'll do what I can to increase patrol presence up here. But those sliding doors are easy to force. You might consider blocking the track with a broom handle."

"I'll take care of it," Aleksy said. "I'll take care of her."

"See that you do." He walked to the door.

"Thank you," Faye said.

"Hey, bro," Aleksy called.

Jarek half-turned.

"Give my love to Tess."

The chief's harsh face relaxed in a smile. "Come to dinner Friday. You can give it to her yourself."

They made quite a picture on their way to the black-and-white cop car—the same dark hair, the same long, muscled backs, the same unconscious arrogance in the set of their shoulders, the same assurance in their strides. Another woman would have drooled. Faye's fingers itched for her sketchbook.

But before the impulse formed into action, Aleksy came back up the walk alone. Faye caught herself admiring the proportions of his chest, the strength of his thighs, and flushed like an art student with her first nude model.

To hide her embarrassment, she asked, "Who's Tess?"

Aleksy pushed open the screen. "Teresa DeLucca. Local reporter. Got herself engaged to Jarek about a month ago."

"You don't approve," she guessed.

"It's not up to me to approve. Jarek seems happy." He wandered toward her kitchen. "Got anything to drink?"

He certainly didn't mind making himself at home, she thought. But he must be thirsty. She wondered how many hours he'd spent on her bank spying today. He smelled like the outdoors, like leaves and sun and sweat.

Faye sighed. One drink, and then she'd send him on his way. "Beer or soda?"

"You keep beer in your refrigerator?"

"It's perfectly legal," she said. "I'm over twenty-one."

He flashed his lethal grin. "You look about sixteen. But that's not what I meant. I pegged you as the designer water and herbal tea type."

At least he hadn't told her she looked twelve. "Do you want the beer or not?"

"Yes, please, teacher."

She tugged open the avocado green refrigerator—a mistake left over from the seventies, like disco or silk shirts for men—and pulled out a long-necked bottle. He thanked her and tipped it back. She tried not to stare at his throat as he swallowed. There was an angry pink sunburn above the collar of his T-shirt. When he stretched his neck, she could see a line of pale, smooth skin below. Her own mouth dried.

Oh, dear. Oh, no.

She hugged her left arm across her chest, holding it like a barrier between them. "Why don't you like your sister-in-law?"

"Future sister-in-law." He set the bottle down on the counter. "And I like Tess fine. We're a lot alike in some ways."

She tried to hear what he was not saying. "Pushy? Stubborn? Obnoxious?"

Aleksy laughed, a warm, rich, surprised sound. "She's not as bad as me. Just…independent."

"Not too independent to get married, apparently."

He picked up his beer. "We'll see."

Faye didn't want to get involved, but this was fascinating stuff. "You don't think she'll go through with it?"

"I think she'll do it. I just hope they can make a success of it. Marriage is a tough proposition."

"What made you such a pessimist?"

He lowered the bottle from his lips. "Experience."

Faye could understand that. She took another beer out of the fridge. Her own mother was currently vacationing in Florida with husband number four. Her father—her mother's second husband—was a self-absorbed academic who had always preferred the company of his books to the demands of a wife and child.

In Faye's life, Aunt Eileen was her biggest constant. Her students were her biggest joy. She closed her eyes a moment, remembering Jamal.

Do not go there.

She turned with her bottle and found herself staring straight into Aleksy's alert brown eyes. Too close. Too aware. Her heart beat up in her throat.

She cleared it. "So, are your parents divorced?"

He smiled knowingly. Well, heavens, the man didn't have to be a detective to see how he affected her. "Nope," he said. "Mom and Pop are solid. We're the ones who keep screwing up."

"We?"

"My brother. His first marriage was a washout. My sister. She'd like to take the plunge but she hasn't managed it yet. And me."

"And have you ever taken the plunge marriage-wise?"

"Hell, no. I'm afraid to even get my feet wet."

Faye looked at him propped against her kitchen counter, his biceps swelling the arms of his shirtsleeves, his legs crossed casually at the ankles, one hundred eighty pounds of tough, hard cop. No one would think of pushing *him* down the stairs. "You don't look afraid of anything."

He winked at her. "It's an act. The cop who isn't afraid of marriage just hasn't looked at the divorce stats."

"Is it the hours?"

"The hours." He shrugged. "The opportunities. A lot of guys think it's a waste not to take what's on offer, married or not."

Faye shook her head. "I tell my students that's a matter of personal responsibility. And if you tell me it's because their wives don't understand them, I want my beer back."

Aleksy looked surprised. And then he smiled. "Come and take it," he invited softly.

She met his hot, dark gaze. Her insides jittered. She wasn't ready... She couldn't possibly... No.

"Never mind. You keep it," she said. "Maybe I just don't understand."

"The only person who can understand what being a cop is like is another cop."

She should leave it alone. She really should.

She didn't.

"Did you ever try dating another cop?"

"I tried. It didn't work out."

"Why not?"

Aleksy turned the bottle in his hands. Buying time for his reply? "She wanted more than I could give. To her or any woman."

Faye could have disliked him for his casual tone, but there was genuine regret in his eyes. "Maybe in time—"

"No."

"There are such things as second chances."

"Yeah? What about you, teacher? Do you believe you get a second chance?"

She flinched. "That's what I'm up here trying to figure out," she said with as much dignity as she could muster. "When you go back to Chicago—"

"It's too late," he interrupted roughly.

"It's never too late," Faye said.

Maybe, in that moment, in the heat of convincing him, she even believed it.

"It is for Karen." He set his empty bottle down hard on the counter. "She's dead."

Chapter 5

Faye's big doe eyes widened in distress.

He could use that, Aleksy thought.

He could use her when he went to pump DeLucca tonight.

The thought left an unaccustomed bad taste in his mouth. What kind of jerk bastard would take advantage of Faye's natural sympathy, would abuse her sweetness and warmth, to get what he wanted?

His kind of jerk bastard. A cop jerk bastard.

"I'm sorry," she said. "Was it recent?"

He moved his shoulders restlessly. "Karen's death? Yeah. Six weeks ago." In a godforsaken warehouse lot in a sting that should never have gone down.

Faye touched his arm. Her fingers were cool from the bottle. He wanted to warm them with his hands. "It hurts," she said. "Losing someone you love."

"I didn't love Karen," he said. Hey, there were limits to how far even he would go. Pretending a lost love to soften Faye up was apparently beyond his. "We were friends. Partners. When things screwed up—when I screwed up things between us—Karen put in for a transfer. Which got her on this high-risk, high-profile task force, which got her killed."

"I'm sorry," Faye said again, like she meant it. Like she didn't hold it against him that he'd busted into her cottage and her life and wrecked her summer vacation.

Aleksy felt guilty. But not so guilty that he didn't press his advantage.

"Thanks." He leaned forward and held her gaze, using his you-can-trust-me voice. "That's what I'm doing up here. Investigating Karen's death."

Faye's lips formed a pretty pink "O." Her pupils dilated. Ah, what the hell, he thought.

"I really appreciate your cooperation," he murmured. He lowered his head.

He was a jerk. He didn't want her cooperation. He wanted to jump her bones.

She took a step back and crossed her arms. "I am not cooperating."

He leered at her. "Not even a little bit?"

"Not even a—" She sighed. "Maybe a little. What do you want?"

He felt his grin broaden.

"Not a chance," she said.

She was so easy, he thought.

"I don't know what you're upset about," he complained. "I just want to use your shower."

"My shower?"

"Yeah. I really need to wash up. I stink."

She didn't argue with that. "You could go home."

"No, I can't. I promised my brother I'd take care of you."

Besides, if things were finally moving on this case, if somebody was rattled enough to break into Faye's cottage and rip off her pictures, the last thing Aleksy wanted was to leave the scene.

Her chin lifted. "Tell him I refused."

"I can't do that."

"Why not?"

"You don't have brothers, do you?"

"I—" She looked adorably confused. "No, I don't."

Cream puff was all alone in the world. It figured. If Aleksy were her brother, he sure wouldn't let some hard-living, fast-talking cop move in on her.

"Trust me on this," he said. "I can't leave you here without protection."

"Why does it matter? Whoever broke in already has whatever he was looking for."

Okay, so she wasn't *that* easy.

"Maybe," he said. "We won't really know until we identify that boat you saw."

"And how are we going to do that?"

"Mark DeLucca—Tess's brother—he knows boats. He tends bar at the Blue Moon. We could catch up with him tonight. Maybe if he saw that sketch of yours, he could give us a better idea of what we're looking for."

She arched her eyebrows. "Unofficially."

Be very unofficial, Jarek had said.

And teacher had paid attention. Aleksy couldn't be sure if that was a good thing or not.

"No point in calling attention to our investigation," he said.

Especially since his lieutenant had specifically forbidden him from any and all involvement in the case.

Faye's big brown eyes considered him. "You want to use my shower."

"Yeah."

"And borrow my sketchbook."

"Please."

She cradled her wrist. "Nothing else?"

"Not a thing." He flashed her a grin. "Well, you could let me buy you a drink tonight."

She didn't smile back. "Why?"

"Payback for the beer?"

She didn't say anything, just stood there regarding him with those wide, dark eyes.

He shrugged. "Maybe I want to thank you."

"Maybe. Or maybe you just want me to provide you with cover."

She was too quick, he thought.

"How about both?" he said.

"All right," she said finally. "But I'm not really involved."

"Of course not."

Aleksy knew he was lying. He wondered if Faye did, too.

Her soap was purple and her shampoo smelled like flowers.

Aleksy grinned as he hung a fluffy green towel on the back of Faye's bathroom door. If anybody in the squad room got a whiff of him now, they'd think he was a pouf.

He yanked on the clean shirt he kept in his car and ran his fingers through his damp hair. Good enough, he thought, checking his look in the mirror. This wasn't a date.

Faye's soft voice echoed in his head. *Or maybe you just want me to provide you with cover.*

His reflection winced. Yeah.

He flipped off the light and left the bathroom. "Hey, Faye!" He strode toward the living room. "You rea—"

He rounded the corner and saw her, and his tongue stuck to the roof of his mouth.

The full, flowered skirt was gone.

The wistful hippie girl was gone.

In her place was a sleek little number in tight dark jeans and a formfitting black top that exposed a lot of soft, smooth chest and an eye-riveting sliver of skin above a heavy leather belt. Long, funky earrings sparkled against her pretty neck. Her blond hair was spiked, and she'd done something to her eyes to make them look big and shadowed. Sexy.

His body went on alert. He was in trouble here.

"Hello," said Aleksy. "Who are you, and what have you done with Goldilocks?"

She laughed, an amused, confident, very female sort of laugh, and all the blood left his brain and rushed to his groin.

"I thought I should change," she said.

"Well, you did." He eyed her up and down. "You look like the kind of girl my brother warned me about."

She raised her chin. "Is that a problem?"

"Not really. I never listened to him, anyway."

She smiled at him uncertainly and the lust inside him twisted and slid into something softer and more dangerous.

Oh, yeah. Very big trouble here.

"Let's go," Aleksy said. "I have to see a man about a boat."

No one would patronize the Blue Moon bar for its artwork, Faye thought. The walls sported a glass-eyed deer and an assortment of brightly lit beer signs. A big stuffed fish, its stretched mouth full of teeth, hung over the bar.

But the view of the lake, coral in the sunset, was breathtaking. And the bartender was gorgeous.

His face had the dark, secretive beauty of a portrait subject from the Italian Renaissance. A Medici, maybe, or a Borgia. His eyes were black. His body was lean and hard.

Faye stared. He was almost perfectly proportioned— long legs, narrow hips, fabulous—

Aleksy took her elbow and nudged her toward a table by the window. "Sit down."

"Is that Mark DeLucca? The bartender?"

"Yeah."

She craned her neck to get another look. "I thought you wanted to talk to him."

"I will. I have to get our drinks."

She tugged her arm from his grasp. "I'll go with you."

"You don't have to."

She was confused. "But I thought you wanted to show him my sketchbook."

"So?"

"Wouldn't it look more natural if I were there?"

Aleksy scowled. "Fine. You can tag along if you promise not to drool in my beer."

She considered being offended; discovered she felt complimented instead. "You're jealous."

"Of what?"

"Of him," she said, pleased with her observation.

Aleksy looked disbelieving. "DeLucca?"

"He's very good looking," Faye said, enjoying his reaction. Skinny art teachers had so few opportunities to play femme fatale. She liked the role. At least for tonight.

Aleksy threaded through the crowded tables. "So's a snake, but I wouldn't want to be one." He leaned against the polished bar until the bartender looked their way. "Mark."

Mark DeLucca jerked his head in acknowledgment. "Alex. What'll it be?"

"Whatever's on draft." Aleksy raised an eyebrow at Faye. She nodded, amused by his possessiveness. "Two."

"Two drafts." Mark reached for and filled two mugs with easy, economical movements. Beneath the sleeve of his black T-shirt, a tattoo rode his right bicep. Faye squinted to read it but she couldn't make it out.

"There you go." He set their beers in front of them. "Anything else?"

"Jarek says you know boats," Aleksy said, a faint challenge in his tone.

"I know some."

"Could you identify one from a drawing?"

Amusement gleamed in those flat, black eyes. "Depends on the drawing."

Aleksy nudged her arm. "Faye?"

That was her cue. She scrambled for her sketchbook, flipped to the right page and laid it on the bar. "This one," she said, laying it open on the bar. "The boat here."

Mark studied it, his brows drawing together over his straight nose. "Could be a Parker Pilothouse," he said after a moment. "The color's right—that kind of off-white beige—and the cabin. Is this drawing to scale?"

Faye stiffened. Maybe she was a little dissatisfied

with her recent work, but she hadn't lost her grasp of the basics. "Yes, of course."

"Okay. So, looking at the dock, your boat's maybe twenty-five feet long. Pointed prow. Yamaha engine?"

"Excuse me?"

One long finger tapped her drawing. "The outboard engine. Was it a Yamaha?"

"I don't remember," she confessed, feeling inadequate again. "It was black."

"Yeah, I can see that. Parker Pilothouse," Mark said to Aleksy. "Late 90s, at a guess. Kind of surprising to find one around here."

"Why is that?" Aleksy asked.

"The manufacturer's down in North Carolina. They only build around six hundred boats a year. Not a custom boat, but nice and fast."

"It would be," Aleksy said grimly. "Storage?"

"Plenty in the V-berth. Why?"

"I can't tell you."

"Suit yourself." Mark wiped his bar and smiled at Faye. "Nice picture. One of yours?"

She smiled back tentatively. "Yes. Thank you."

"You the artist who took the Harper cottage for the summer?"

"Why, yes. Eileen Harper is my aunt. I used to visit her sometimes when I was growing up. For an entire summer, once, when I was fourteen."

"Summer girl, huh?"

Something about the way he said it made her defensive. "Maybe to you. I always felt like I belonged here."

"We won't keep you," Aleksy said. "Thanks for the help."

"Anytime," Mark said blandly.

Aleksy picked up both beers and started across the tiny, scarred dance floor.

"Nice meeting you," Faye called over her shoulder.

On the jukebox, Donna Summer yielded to the theme from *Hawaii Five-O*. Faye grinned as she trailed Aleksy to a booth at the back. It was too funny. Too perfect. She already felt like an unpaid extra in a bad police drama.

"So, what was that about?" she asked after they were seated.

Aleksy angled to face the door. "I can't discuss an ongoing police investigation with Mark DeLucca."

Oh, really. "We weren't discussing your investigation. We were talking about my painting."

A gleam entered his coffee dark eyes. "So, talk."

Oh, dear. "You don't want to talk about my painting."

"How do you know?"

"You never said anything about my work before."

And it stung.

"Maybe I didn't want to sound dumb."

"Yes, I can see that insecurity is a problem for you," she said dryly.

He laughed. "Is it for you?"

Yes.

She traced the condensation on her glass with her finger. "I suppose all artists want approval to some degree."

He leaned back in his seat. "So, what do you want? You want me to tell you I like your stuff?"

Her heart beat faster. She gulped her beer. "I want you to tell me what you think," she said firmly.

Well, unless he hated it.

Aleksy took her open sketchbook by the edge and

turned it around. She tried not to fidget as he thumbed slowly through the pages—sky, bank, water, woods, viridian and blue, sienna and gray.

"Pretty," he said at last, and closed the book.

That was it? She had hours, days, weeks of work in there.

"Thank you," she said.

He watched her steadily. "You're disappointed."

"No." She bit her lip on the lie. "Maybe I hoped you'd be... I don't know."

"More perceptive?"

"More—" *interested* "—impressed."

"Sweetheart, I have to use a ruler and a compass to draw an accurate crime scene. Believe me, I'm impressed."

"Art's not about accuracy. It's supposed to evoke an emotional response."

He grinned. "Yeah, well, the D.A. gets very emotional over badly drawn crime scenes."

Faye tried to work up a little indignation. But it was tough with Aleksy sitting across the table, strong and reassuring, a grin on his lips and an invitation in his eyes.

"Philistine," she said, without heat.

"I told you I didn't know anything about art."

"But you know how you feel."

He shrugged. "Sure."

"And my work doesn't make you feel anything."

"What do you want? I said it was pretty."

Right. What *did* she want? She painted pretty. She wanted soothing. Didn't she?

She took another sip of beer, her second that day. She was turning into a real wild woman.

"You should see what I was painting six months ago," she said.

"It wasn't pretty?"

"Some of it was." She defended her work. "Well, not pretty. Vibrant. Dynamic."

"Bragging, teacher?"

"No, I—" She smiled. "Maybe I am."

Aleksy looked at her, his expression arrested. "You should do that more often."

Her laughter spurted out. "Brag?"

"Smile."

She was vaguely offended. And maybe just a little drunk. "I smile."

"Not a lot."

Two beers. She'd only had two beers. "Well, excuse me. I just had my home broken into. Maybe I don't have a lot to smile about."

He watched her across the scarred and darkened table. "I could help you with that."

"With the break-in? You already—"

"No." His eyes were hot and steady. "Let me take you home and see if I can give you something to smile about."

Faye's mouth gaped. She must look like that fish over the bar. She closed it. Opened it. Asked, "Are you out of your mind?"

"Nope. I don't think so."

"You barely know me."

"I know enough."

"Enough for what?"

Aleksy smiled, all male confidence. She felt the heat spread low in her stomach and in her cheeks. "Don't answer that," she said hastily.

"Okay."

He sounded agreeable. Relaxed.

Frustrated, tempted, she glared at him, at the coiled energy in his chest and arms, at his long hands restlessly turning his glass. Not so relaxed after all, she thought. Good.

"It wouldn't work," she said.

"Why not?"

"I need to know someone better before I... I need to know you better."

"Let me take you home," he said again. "I guarantee you'll know me better."

Her lungs emptied of breath. Her mind emptied of thought. There was a part of her, a large and surprisingly vocal part, that wanted to say yes.

Maybe it was the beer.

Or maybe it was him, tough cop Aleksy Denko. He was warm and vital and fearless, and she was sick of being alone and safe and sad.

Tonight, at least, she wanted to wrap herself in his heat. She wanted to absorb some of his energy, borrow a little of his confidence. She wanted to rub up, quite literally, against danger.

The realization panicked her.

"That would be—" Wonderful, she thought. Reckless. Exciting. "—a very bad idea," she said.

"Are you sure?" he asked softly.

A lot of guys think it's a waste not to take what's on offer, married or not.

"Yes," she said.

He shrugged and slid her a crooked smile that snagged her like a fishhook. "You can't blame a guy for trying."

"That depends. How often do you try?"

"You want a list of prior sexual partners?"

"How about a clean bill of health?" She felt her face heat to scarlet. "I'm sorry. That was unnecessary."

"Maybe not," he drawled, and her flush deepened.

If they became lovers, he meant.

"It was still rude," she said.

"It was smart," he corrected. "A good detective decides cases on the evidence."

"I'm not a detective."

"No." The warmth in his eyes made her heart stutter. "But I like you anyway."

Maybe she liked him, too.

Bruce Springsteen took over the jukebox. Under the cover of music, they talked, getting-to-know-you stuff about favorite parks and who made the best pizza in Chicago.

Faye finished her beer, which may have been a mistake, but she wasn't driving. She waved to Mark De-Lucca as they left the bar. She didn't have to worry about getting mugged in the parking lot, either. Not with the virile Detective Dynamite at her side. The thought made her giggle.

Aleksy narrowed his eyes at her. "How much have you had to drink?"

"Two beers."

"That's all?"

"I'm small. And I didn't eat much." She swayed toward him in challenge. "Are you going to make me take a Breathalyzer test?"

"No. I'm going to pour you into the car and take you home."

"Okay." She leaned against the padded headrest and drifted through the starlit drive, feeling relaxed and cared for.

Aleksy opened her door and escorted her up the walk.

"Key?" he ordered at her door.

She dug it out of her bag and handed it over. He left her on the lit porch while he did a quick search of the inside.

Checking for intruders, she realized. A little of her well-being leaked away.

Returning, Aleksy steered her inside and closed the door behind him. The click of the lock prodded her to full awareness. Somewhere along the way he'd retrieved his bag from the bathroom and parked it under an end table.

She sobered fast. "You're not staying here."

Aleksy heard the edge in her voice. He had to back off, or he was going to lose her.

"Relax, cream puff. I'll sleep on the couch."

"No. We agreed—"

"Whoever ripped you off thinks you're here alone. I'd like them to see my car parked in your driveway overnight."

"Why? They weren't looking for proof that you're living here. They were after the photos."

Damn. She was back in teacher mode. Loose and woozy would have made things easier on both of them. Not that he would have taken advantage of her drunken state to get any closer than her couch... At least, he didn't think he would. He wanted her willing in bed. And he needed her compliance on this case.

"*Maybe* they were after the photos," he said.

"And they got them."

"And this makes you feel better?"

"Yes." Her little chin stuck out. "If they already have what they want, I'm safe."

He forced himself not to yell at her. "Only if you take reasonable precautions."

"Since when is letting a strange man sleep on my couch a reasonable precaution?"

"Since they broke into your house. Faye, these bastards are already responsible for one woman's death. I need to be here. That way if they try anything else, I'm in a position to protect you."

"And catch them."

Wasn't that what the good guys were supposed to do? Although in this case, his hands were tied until he had more evidence.

"If it comes to that, yeah. Otherwise, I'll just be here to keep an eye on things."

She crossed her arms under her small, perfect breasts. "Is that why you put the moves on me earlier? So you'd be here to keep an eye on things?"

Hell.

"No."

Maybe.

He used his discomfort to fuel the heat in his voice. "Come on, Faye. You don't think I find you attractive?"

"I think you find me convenient. I think you'd do anything to bring your Karen's murderers to justice." Her big brown eyes were clear and hurt. "Including lie to me."

Yes.

It was a lousy admission to take to bed. Especially since he figured that if things had only been different—if *he* had only been different—he might have had Faye instead.

Chapter 6

"Would you like coffee?" Faye asked politely the next morning as Aleksy came out of the bathroom.

Whoa. And a howdy good morning to *you*. His body, still warm from sleep and heavy from a lingering dream, reacted fiercely to the sight of her—her messy blond hair, her pale, nude lips, her bare, arched feet. He wanted to back her through her bedroom door and flat onto her mattress.

He met her eyes. *Not going to happen,* they announced. *Not in a million years.*

He cleared his throat. "Coffee would be great. Thanks."

He followed her to the kitchen, with its solid cabinets and outdated appliances, and leaned against the counter as she scooped grounds into a paper filter. She was such a cream puff. Soft and sweet. Even pissed, she couldn't resist taking care of him. He bet her students loved her.

He frowned as he thought of that kid, that Jamal, who

had loved her and given her such grief. Taken such advantage of her.

The way Aleksy was doing.

The thought made him uncomfortable.

It wasn't the same, Aleksy told himself as the coffee-maker bubbled and spat. He was just doing his job. Well, not his job, exactly. His lieutenant had ordered him to stay off the case.

"How much longer do you plan to stay?" Faye asked, handing him a cup.

The full mug burned his hand. He shifted his grip to the handle. "That depends on how long you need protection."

"Please. You're not going to stand there and tell me that every break-in victim warrants twenty-four hour police protection. How long?"

I think you'd do anything... Including lie to me.

The memory chafed like an over-starched uniform collar.

"That depends," he hedged.

"On what?"

"On whether I can establish a connection between the boat you drew and the guy I'm after. I'm not working alone on this." Hell, he wasn't supposed to be working this case at all. "Other detectives—other agencies—are trying to trace the money angle. Checking phone records. Chasing trucks across the border. All I can do is sit and wait for something to happen."

Her eyes widened. "What is it these men are supposed to have done?"

If he told her, she would immediately understand his interest in Dick Freer. And that would put her and his investigation at risk.

"You don't need to know," he said.

"But you still want me to help."

He gave her a crooked smile. Could she be charmed? "Yeah."

She studied the steam rising from her mug. "We'd need different sleeping arrangements," she said abruptly.

Oh, yeah. Absolutely. He wished she would look at him.

"What side of the bed do you want?" he asked.

Her gaze jerked to his. Her face flooded with color. "Never mind. It would never work," she said.

"Sure it will," he countered. She wasn't pretending offense, he saw. There was real distress in her eyes. "It was a joke. A bad joke. What did you have in mind?"

"I can't have you sleeping in my work space. It's too—" she hesitated "—distracting."

Her admission soothed his ego. Provoked his libido. But after her reaction to his earlier crack, he wasn't going to risk another sexual remark.

"Okay, so the couch isn't working," he said. "There's always the bathtub."

Her lips curved. Reluctantly, he thought. "I don't think that would work, either. There is a back bedroom. I've used it—oh, years ago."

"That's convenient."

"Not really. Aunt Eileen's been using it for storage. But you could have a look at it."

"Great."

She still looked doubtful. "It's kind of a mess."

He smiled encouragement. "How bad can it be?"

"It's bad," Aleksy acknowledged to his brother twenty-eight hours later.

"Do you need backup?" Jarek asked instantly.

Aleksy wedged the phone under his jaw and shut off the water. "No. It's not the case. It's living here. With her."

There was a breath on the other end of the line that might have been exasperation. Or laughter. "What, the art teacher has you shackled to the bed now?"

"No. We've got separate rooms."

But he could still smell her scent, that light mix of flowers and soap, every time she walked by.

He could still hear her humming tunelessly in the shower.

He still had to watch her padding around barefoot in her skimpy summer tops and scanty underwear.

A glass slipped from Aleksy's hand into the soapy water. Actually, he'd only caught her once in her underwear, pale smooth cotton that rode high on her slender legs and low on her gently curved belly.

"So, what's the problem?" Jarek asked.

"The problem is—" The memory of Faye in her underwear had momentarily wiped the problem from his mind. He shook his head to clear it. "I'm just not used to the whole living together scene, you know? I mean, the last time I had to look at yogurt in the fridge, I was home with Mom and Nora."

"Yogurt seems a small price to pay for a comfortable crib with an unrestricted view of your suspect."

Not to mention the other views he was getting, Aleksy thought.

He rinsed the glass. "I guess you're right."

"You don't really have a problem until you start eating the yogurt," Jarek teased.

Aleksy stared, stricken, at the refrigerator.

"Alex?"

"I only tasted it," he said defensively. "She put stuff in it, berries and stuff. I didn't want to be rude."

"You ate her yogurt." His brother's voice was nearly expressionless.

That was it. When Aleksy saw Jarek again, he would have to kill him.

"I could have handled it if she made a big production out of mealtimes. You know, the wine and candlelight routine. *Honey, I made waffles and let's take the syrup back to bed?* Only she doesn't. But every time I get hungry, she's already got something going in the kitchen. Good food. Nothing fancy. And she tells me what she's working on, or stories about her students, and—" He realized how much he was betraying and shut up. "Jare, I'm dying here."

"Regular meals in agreeable company. Yeah, I can see how that would hurt."

"You don't get it. Since you got yourself engaged to the reporter babe, you've completely lost perspective."

"Looks like it," Jarek agreed. He didn't even sound upset. "See you at seven?"

"What's at seven?"

"Friday. Dinner? Tess is cooking."

Aleksy swished the big sandwich knife in the water and set it on the drain board. "Thanks for the warning."

"You better show, or you'll get more than a warning."

"That woman's got you whipped, bro."

"Yeah? What are you doing right now, hotshot?"

Aleksy jerked his hands out of the soapy water. When they were kids, and later, when he'd followed Jarek on to the force, he used to suspect his older brother of possessing some kind of super power deductive skill. Now he was sure of it.

"I'm just marking time," he said. "Until something breaks on the case."

"Sure," said Jarek.

Aleksy scowled. "Did you check out the registration on that boat?"

"Yeah, I passed it on to some guys I know." After twenty years on the Chicago force, the guys Jarek knew made up a Who's Who of law enforcement in the Midwest. "They'll get back to me. I might even have an answer for you tonight."

Something inside him relaxed. "Great. Okay. I'll see you at seven."

"Bring the teacher if you want," his brother said.

Aleksy couldn't do that. A date for family dinner? It would make them seem too much like a couple.

He wasn't even getting any.

"I'll ask her," he said.

Anyway, she'd say no. Faye didn't want an involvement any more than he did.

After he hung up, he went looking for her but she wasn't at her worktable or in her bedroom or on the deck. Which had to mean she'd gone to collect the mail without telling him.

His scowl deepened. It was a good thing he had exaggerated her possible danger. If the bad guys were really after Faye she'd be dead by now.

He stalked to the screen and glared toward the road. Nothing.

She was fine.

Of course she was fine.

A minute ticked by, marked by the shadow of a cloud creeping down the drive and the distant roar of a powerboat. Two minutes. Five.

Aleksy swore and jammed the mop handle into the

sliding door. He pocketed a key to the cottage and started down the pine-strewn driveway. She was fine. At least until he caught up with her and told her what he thought of her for worrying him like this.

Faye was sitting on a flat rock by the side of the gravel drive, her skirt collapsed around her, envelopes and circulars scattered beside her. Her arms clasped her knees; her pale face lifted to the sun. She'd picked a hell of a time to get a tan.

Relief burst in Aleksy's gut and made him angry, like that time his six-year-old niece had slipped away from him in the grocery store and he'd found her in front of the ice cream. His jaw clenched. Of all the stupid, inconsiderate—

He stopped in his tracks.

She was crying. Silently, with her eyes closed, but definitely crying all the same. Now that he was closer, he could see the shine of tears on her cheeks. Her lips were parted. Her nose was red.

Panic time. He didn't "do" crying any better than he did commitment.

Her wet lashes lifted. Her desolate gaze socked him like a fist in the chest. Aleksy forgot about what he did and didn't do and went to sit beside her on the rock.

Faye just opened her eyes and he was there, conjured out of her sorrow and her need, a big, dark, annoyed-looking antidote to grief and guilt.

She was so glad to see him she felt the tears well again. She squeezed her lids shut.

But she heard him move, the crunch of boots on gravel. She felt him settle beside her, the brush of his thigh, the solid warmth of his shoulder. She smelled him, clean and male and reassuring.

"So, who died?" he asked.

Her eyes popped open. Her jaw dropped. "That is about the most insensitive thing I've ever heard anyone say."

"You want sensitive, call a girlfriend. You want concerned, I'm here." He swiveled his head to look at her directly and her heart gave a funny bump. "I worried when you didn't come back to the house."

The tension left her shoulders. "I'm sorry."

"Next time you're going to disappear, say something."

"I will. I didn't plan to be gone so long."

"Yeah, I figured." His long legs stretched out in front of them, muscle wrapped in denim. He nodded toward the mail slipping away across the rock. "What happened? You get bad news?"

Her throat constricted. She swallowed. "In a manner of speaking."

His attention sharpened. "Threats?"

"No! No, nothing like that."

He waited.

She sighed. "I heard from a former student, that's all."

"Jamal?"

"How—" He was a detective, she reminded herself. He had an eye for detail and a good memory. "Yes. Jamal King."

"What he do this time? Send you a postcard of the Grand Canyon?"

She smiled reluctantly. "He sent me a sketch."

Aleksy held out his hand.

Wordlessly she passed him the envelope Jamal had

constructed from two pieces of cardboard taped together. Someone at school must have given him her address—although it was a good bet Principal Carter would not have approved.

Aleksy found the slit in the tape and eased out the single sheet of art paper.

She didn't bother to look at it. The picture was already clear in her brain. The memory was fresh in her heart.

Jamal had made the colored ink drawing last fall when the two of them were working after school in the studio, before everything had gone so disastrously wrong. In the sketch, she was painting—what? Faye didn't remember now and Jamal's sketch didn't show. But the picture clearly revealed both Faye's own absorption in her work and the young artist's affection for his teacher/subject.

Jamal's quick pen and sensitive use of color had captured that golden afternoon more evocatively than any photograph—the sun-drenched room, the play of light on the cluttered tables, Faye's energy and hope.

"Damn," said Aleksy.

It was a tribute and Faye accepted it as such. "Jamal is very talented."

"I don't know talented, but he sure caught you. Why wouldn't he keep this? Or sell it?"

"He did keep it for a while. He made this sketch last October."

"Then why send it to you now?"

"I don't know." She pleated her skirt between her fingers. "I'm afraid it's a cry for help."

"You think he's in trouble," Aleksy stated.

"Yes."

"He was a good kid, you said. 'Not a problem.'"

"No. But—" She stopped. No matter how sympathetic Aleksy seemed, he was a law enforcement officer. She couldn't bear it if she said anything that got Jamal in deeper trouble.

"His parents' expectations put him under a lot of stress," she said carefully. "He might have made some…unwise choices."

"You think he'd hurt somebody?"

Oh, dear. "Oh, no. But he could hurt himself."

"Suicide? Or drugs?"

She winced. So much for being careful. "I wondered at the end of fall quarter," she said. "I knew he wasn't getting enough sleep, and I thought he'd lost some weight. But when I asked him about using drugs, he told me it was just the pressure of finals. He really wanted to do well. And he seemed to get better, in January. But after that everything fell apart."

"He turned down that art scholarship, you mean."

"He turned down the scholarship, and—" oh, it still hurt "—his parents withdrew him from my class."

"Getting yanked from art class doesn't turn most kids into speed freaks."

"Jamal is not most kids," Faye said fiercely. "He was better than any other student I had. Better than me. He had a true gift."

"And he decided not to use it. It was his decision, right? I mean, the kid must be, what, sixteen? Seventeen?"

"Seventeen."

"Old enough to stand up to his parents, then. If that was what he really wanted."

"Is that what you did at seventeen?" she challenged.

He shrugged. "Sure. Maybe not so dramatically. Art schools weren't exactly lining up to give me money.

But at that age, I already knew I wanted to follow Jarek on to the force. And our folks were equally certain they didn't want both of their sons getting shot at for a living. So there was some conflict there.''

"*Some* conflict," Faye repeated. "Did they call you stupid and ungrateful for not taking advantage of the opportunities they had sacrificed to provide you with? Did they tell you you were letting your little brother and sisters down? Did they threaten to throw you out of the house unless you went along with what they wanted?''

"No," he said slowly. "We disagreed, but I knew Mom and Pop were always in my corner.''

"You were lucky, then. Jamal didn't have anybody in his corner.''

Aleksy's eyes were dark and unreadable. "Except you.''

"Except me," Faye agreed bleakly. "And I only made things worse.''

"So why do you think he'd reach out to you now?''

She hugged her knees. "I don't know.''

"You could be reading too much into this. Maybe the kid was just cleaning out his desk. Maybe he wanted to let you know he's all right.''

He was trying to reassure her. She was grateful. But she didn't believe him for a moment.

Aleksy hadn't watched Jamal give up what he loved to fit the school administration's profile of a good student, to follow his parents' plans for their good child.

He hadn't stood helplessly by as the boy's creative energy was driven underground and became anger.

He hadn't observed Jamal's increasing irritability, the crashing lows and sometimes manic highs that characterized a kid on the edge—or an amphetamine addict.

Aleksy didn't know and Faye wasn't going to tell him. Her last attempt to tell had done enough damage.

"I hope that's it," she said. "Thank you."

Aleksy frowned. "Look, I know a couple of cops in the Juvenile Division. I could talk to them, maybe get a word on your kid."

"No. I don't want you to go to any—"

"It's no trouble."

"It's not your problem," she insisted.

"You're helping me out. Let me help you."

He sounded sincere. He looked hard and capable. Even relaxed against the rock with stubble shadowing his jaw and the sun finding highlights in his hair, he looked like a cop. He didn't need the star in his pocket or the gun hidden at his back to give him authority.

If she let herself believe him...

If she let herself believe...

Her gaze fell to the sketch in Aleksy's hand. A cry for help, she had called it. If Jamal were in trouble— serious trouble, *police* trouble—wouldn't it be better if Aleksy were involved?

But Faye's belief had been badly shaken in the past three months. She no longer trusted the authorities or her own judgment. She had lost her faith that things would always work out.

What if she told Aleksy her suspicions and made things worse for Jamal?

"I don't need your help," she said.

She was lying. Or hiding something.

Aleksy had conducted too many interrogations to miss the defensive set of her shoulders, the betraying flicker of her lashes.

He wanted to protest. He wanted to help. She could trust him.

But the assurances went flat and sour in his mouth, like a beer that stood open too long.

Trust him?

Could she really?

He hadn't lied to her—well, except about his having an official role in this investigation. But he hadn't told her the whole truth, either.

He was using her. Not the way he used most women, not for laughs or recreational sex, to take the physical edge off loneliness. But using her all the same.

His mother, Mary Denko, would have been ashamed of him. Aleksy was disconcerted to discover he was a little ashamed himself.

"If you won't let me put out a feeler on the kid, you have to let me do something."

Faye turned her head to look at him. "Why?"

"Because—"

Because he felt guilty, damn it.

Because despite her claim not to need him, he had seen tears on her eyelashes, and they scorched his heart. The pixie art teacher was caring and dedicated, qualities he respected. She deserved more thanks than a sketch in the mail. More support than an absentee aunt and an empty vacation cottage could provide.

"I owe you for lunch," he said.

"You did the dishes."

"I still owe you. I don't want to take advantage."

Much.

Just let me into your home, sweetheart, so I can spy on the bad guys and maybe get a look at you in your pretty panties. Let me into your confidence.

Let me into your bed.

She lifted one slim shoulder. "Fine. You can make dinner."

It took him a second to drag his dirty mind from the vision of her smooth, bare thighs and naked stomach.

"Right," he said. "Dinner. I can—" Memory smacked him. Oh, damn. "I have a conflict."

Her lips curved. "You can't cook?"

"I can cook. But I promised my brother I'd eat at his place tonight."

"Another time, then." Was he imagining it or did she sound disappointed?

"You could come," he said.

"Thank you, but I'm sure your brother—"

"Jarek invited you."

And, boy, would he be surprised to see her. Aleksy never brought his lovelies home to meet the family. His mother wanted more grandchildren. The women wanted—well, despite Aleksy's warnings, some of the women were after more than a good time. Why create expectations he had no intention of satisfying?

"That was kind of him," Faye said politely. "But I'll be fine."

Aleksy didn't want to leave her alone. "You should come." And then, so she didn't get the wrong idea, he added, "For your own protection."

She wasn't impressed. "Nothing's happened since the break-in. I think I'll survive one night on my own."

"For my protection, then," Aleksy said desperately.

"You don't need protection."

"You haven't met Tess," he said.

Faye's eyes lit with amusement. Deliberately he held her gaze until the amusement shimmered into something else, until the moment stretched bright and tantalizing between them.

"Come to dinner at my brother's," he commanded softly. "Please?"

Her throat moved. "All right. If you're sure it's okay."

He wasn't sure of anything, except that his brother was absolutely going to razz him about this.

But staring into Faye's warm brown gaze, Aleksy couldn't help feeling that everything was suddenly, incredibly, better than okay.

Chapter 7

Faye stood on the police chief's doorstep feeling as out of place as a trick-or-treater in July. She didn't know these people. She did not want to be involved with this man. And she was pretty sure her skirt and scooped neck T-shirt were wrong, even for a casual family dinner.

"What did you tell them?" she asked Aleksy.

He reached over her shoulder to jam a finger on the bell. "What do you think? I told them I was bringing a date."

"Oh, like your sister-in-law would believe that."

"She's not my sister-in-law yet." Aleksy slanted a look at her. "Why wouldn't she believe it?"

Because any woman in her right mind would immediately recognize that Aleksy Denko belonged with prime babe material. Someone beautiful and sleek. Someone who knew the score. Faye wasn't even sure what game they were playing.

"Because we're not—I'm not your type, remember?" she said.

"It doesn't matter," he said. "Jarek knows who you are."

He didn't disagree with her, she noticed.

"So he'll tell her—what? I had to come to dinner because I'm in protective custody?"

Aleksy drilled the bell again. "Other way around, cream puff. You're protecting me, remember?"

"Oh, please. I can't believe you need protection from—"

The door opened. The woman framed between the white posts was intimidatingly gorgeous, dark and exotic, with big gold earrings and wide gold eyes.

"Hi. You must be Faye." She held out a beautifully manicured hand, her nails a deep, glowing red. "I'm Tess DeLucca."

The bartender's sister. Faye could see the resemblance: those strong, arched brows, that straight, bold nose...

She shook hands. "I met your brother."

Tess stepped back to admit them both into the house. "Well, come in and meet the rest of the family."

"Um," said Faye.

Aleksy's hand touched her back in reassurance. "You already know Jarek."

"Aleksy!" a cheerful voice boomed from inside the house. "You are late."

Aleksy looked at Tess. "You didn't tell me Mom and Pop were going to be here."

She shrugged. "They decided to drive down this afternoon."

"So, come in, come in." A short, handsome, graying

man appeared over her shoulder. "I want to meet your lady friend."

"You always want to meet the ladies." The older woman who entered the hall behind him had Jarek's faint smile and Aleksy's dark eyes. "Sit down and let Tess greet her guests properly."

"Why don't we all sit down?" Tess said, moving back to admit them. "Faye?"

Faye flinched under the impact of two pairs of interested eyes.

"Go get 'em, cream puff," Aleksy murmured behind her.

She threw him an annoyed look and stepped over the threshold.

Aleksy leaned past her to kiss his mother on the cheek. "Hi, Mom. Where's Jare?"

"In the kitchen with Allie, cutting up carrots for the salad," Tess said.

"Didn't trust you with the knife, huh?"

The older man thumped his son on the shoulder. "Manners. Aren't you going to introduce us?"

"Sure, Pop. This is Faye Harper. Faye, my parents, Eric and Mary Denko."

"It's nice to meet you," Faye said politely.

Eric Denko had a broad face, broad hands and a barrel chest. One of the hands engulfed hers. The face split in a smile. "It is very nice to meet you, too. Aleksy, he's not so much interested in girls lately."

Tess snickered.

"Thanks, Pop," Aleksy said.

"I meant, since your friend, that Karen, died," Eric said with dignity.

"She was a nice woman," Mary said. "It was too bad things did not work out between you."

"It happens with partners sometimes," Aleksy said.

"Yes, if one of them maybe wants to be something more than partners," Eric said.

"I'll bet," Tess said. She sounded fascinated.

Faye was pretty fascinated herself. But Aleksy's jaw was tight and his eyes were stormy.

She cleared her throat. "Something smells delicious."

"My chicken paprikas," Mary said. "I teach Tess."

Tess laughed. "Maybe we should say you're *trying* to teach me. Why don't you all get comfortable in the living room, and I'll fetch Jarek and drinks."

"I can get him," Aleksy said. He strode through the arched doorway to the kitchen.

Faye stared after him, torn between concern for his feelings and loss at his desertion.

Tess dropped onto the couch. "He hates it when I make him feel like a guest."

"Which makes it just about irresistible to try," Faye guessed.

Tess grinned. "Oh, you're good. Come sit by me."

Mary settled on a chair and clasped her hands together in her lap. "Jarek said you're a teacher?"

"Well, yes," Faye said, and changed the subject. "Who is Allie?"

"Our Jarek's daughter," Eric said.

"Tess's daughter, soon," Mary said with evident pleasure.

"So, how do you like living with the Boy Scout?" Tess asked.

Faye was used to the gossip in the teachers' lounge, but this tag team interrogation felt different somehow. Friendly. Affectionate. Intimate, even. Was it Tess's training as a reporter? Small town camaraderie? Or family concern? How much did they know of Aleksy's real reasons for staying in her cottage?

She felt like an imposter.

"You brought a *date?*" A girl's voice, high and carrying, floated from the direction of the kitchen. "Jeez, Uncle Alex, is, like, everybody getting married now?"

A male rumble silenced her but it was too late to stop Faye's hot blush.

Tess winced in apology. "That would be Allie. Great kid, big mouth."

"Runs in the family," Aleksy said.

He stood in the doorway, thumbs in his belt loops, taking in the situation and Faye with a glance. She refused to admit, even to herself, how bolstered she felt by his quick, warm appraisal.

"Oh, yeah," Tess said. "You and Jarek are such chatterboxes."

Aleksy grinned. "We talk."

Tess snorted. "To each other, maybe."

"Hey, we're guys."

"They're cops," Tess told Faye. "That's even worse. Heaven help any woman who wants to know what's going on inside those thick skulls."

"Something to drink?" Jarek Denko blocked the arch, carrying a tray of bottles and glasses. Faye was unprepared for the way Tess's bold, clever face softened and glowed at the sight of him.

"Are you going to let her talk about us like that?" Aleksy appealed to his brother.

"I never stop Tess from expressing her opinion. She'll quote the First Amendment at me." Jarek's lake gray eyes warmed as he regarded the woman curled on the couch. "Besides, she's usually right."

"Thick-skulled cops?" Aleksy repeated.

Jarek shrugged and set the tray on the coffee table. "Be grateful she didn't call us boneheaded Polacks."

"Language," Mary said mildly.

Eric laughed.

A slim, dark-haired girl with brand-new sneakers and Jarek's eyes wandered into the room. Allie, Faye presumed.

"Who's a boneheaded Polack?" the girl asked.

"You're a boneheaded Polack," Aleksy said, and grabbed her around the waist. He rubbed his knuckles against her scalp while she laughed and shrieked and protested.

"Mind the drinks," Jarek said, sounding so much like Mary Denko that Faye smiled.

She could like him, she thought, as Aleksy released his knuckle-hold on his niece and the talk became general. She could like them all. She listened, amused and intrigued, as the conversation hopped and flowed from the need for a new traffic light to Tess's hunt for a wedding gown to Allie's chances on making the middle school basketball team in the fall.

The Denko brothers were tough men in a dangerous profession. But it was significant—and very sweet—that top cop Jarek Denko held hands with Tess on the couch. Aleksy, even as he argued with his brother about Eden's need for more female officers, played cards on the floor with his niece.

The talk skipped again to the previous night's game against Minnesota. Jarek and his father followed the Cubs, Aleksy was a White Socks fan—although, after listening to them wrangle, Faye suspected his support had as much to do with a love of argument as the sport of baseball.

He leaned his back against Faye's chair. His shoulder

brushed her knee. His warm hand wrapped around her ankle and her pulse jumped.

He tilted his head to look at her. "You look like you're sizing us all up to put in one of your pictures."

His hair was soft against her arm. From this angle, his eyes were upside down and dangerously charming.

Faye shook her head. "I don't think I could. I haven't figured out how you all fit together yet."

He grinned wickedly. His hand slid a little way up her calf. Her skin tingled at the brush of his fingers, the breadth of his palm.

"I fit fine where I am now."

Her breath caught. Oh.

"Gin," Allie said with satisfaction, spreading her cards on the carpet. "And serves you right, Uncle Alex, for not paying attention."

Tess laughed.

Faye adjusted the long folds of her skirt.

"You cheated," Aleksy said without heat.

Jarek studied the hand laid out on the floor. "Nope. She's got you."

Allie bounced to her knees and brushed the cards together. "Want to play again?"

Aleksy pretended to scowl. "Don't you have to go cook dinner or something?"

"No. It's Tess's turn tonight."

"Swell."

The girl's brows drew together. "She made paprikas. Baba taught her. It's good."

Her solemn defense of her future stepmother touched Faye. It had some effect on Aleksy, too, because he flicked her nose and said, "I bet you're right."

Tess uncurled from the couch. "Speaking of dinner, I should go stir the pot. Want to come?"

Faye almost stood before she realized the question was directed at Allie.

"Eric, you and I will set the table," Mary said firmly, and led her husband from the room.

Aleksy watched them all leave. And then his head swiveled toward his brother. "What did you get on the boat?"

Faye's stomach jerked and clenched. She was still enjoying the illusion of family dinner, the solid feel of Aleksy's back against her legs, the kiss of his hair against her arm. She didn't want to be reminded it was all an act.

But her mild-mannered host wore his police chief face, cool and focused.

"It doesn't belong to your suspect. In fact, that boat doesn't belong to any of the residents on the lake. Which doesn't rule out the possibility that some innocent boat headed from Chicago hauled it up for the weekend."

"Except that a weekend sailor wouldn't have any reason to break into Faye's cottage and steal her painting and photographs."

Jarek smiled thinly. "Maybe not. I checked with the manufacturer in North Carolina. The majority of their sales are along the east coast. There is no Great Lakes distributor. Which means anyone around here with a Parker Pilothouse bought it used or got it direct from the manufacturer."

Aleksy's head came up. "How far back do they keep sales records?"

"Thirty years," Jarek said with satisfaction. "As long as they've been in the business."

"Okay. You've got something. Let's have it."

"Now?" Jarek looked at Faye. "You sure you don't want to talk about this later?"

Later, as in not in front of her.

Faye picked up her wineglass. "I think I'll see if they need help in the kitchen."

Aleksy's hand tightened around her ankle. "It's okay. Who bought the boat?"

"There's no evidence that it's the same boat. But Parker has records of a sale made to a buyer in Toronto four years ago."

Aleksy's eyes narrowed. "What buyer?"

"Later for that."

The two men exchanged another glance.

"Right," said Aleksy. "Tell me how a boat from Toronto ends up on a lake in Illinois."

"Well, it could have changed hands in a private sale."

"That's no help."

"Or the owner could have sailed from Lake Huron into Lake Michigan through the Straits of Mackinac—"

"Under the nose of the Coast Guard?"

"I've been told it could be done. In a small, fast boat."

"Like the Parker Pilothouse."

Jarek nodded. "For example. Anyway, from Lake Michigan, the owner could strike directly for Chicago. Or head south. There are a couple of man-made water diversions there connecting the lake with the Des Plaines and Mississippi rivers. Or he could take his boat upstream on the Jordan River."

"Which goes where?"

Jarek smiled tightly. "Here."

"Then we have our connection," Aleksy said.

"Not quite," Jarek said. "I checked with the Coast

Guard and the bureau's field office. Without a registration number, we don't have probable cause linking this boat to the buyer in Toronto. And without the photographs, there's no proof that it was ever even here.''

Faye fought a shiver. "Unless he comes back."

Jarek spared her a brief, sympathetic glance. "Unless he comes back *and* we can prove he isn't here on legitimate business."

Aleksy's face was grim. His voice was hard. "Oh, I'll get proof," he said.

"Be careful how," Jarek warned. "You don't have a warrant. It's not even your—" A glance from Aleksy silenced him.

Faye's fingers tightened around the stem of her wineglass. Not even his *what?*

"Can you get evidence without a warrant?" she asked.

Aleksy shrugged. "You can get anything you want. Whether you can use it is something else."

"Fruit of the poison tree," Jarek murmured.

She didn't understand them. She didn't even speak the same language. "What fruit? What tree?"

"If an investigating officer violates procedure, the evidence he obtains can be ruled inadmissible by the court," Aleksy explained.

She nodded to show she understood. "So what will you do?"

"Well." He hesitated. "If somebody not directly connected with the investigation—call him a concerned citizen—obtained the same evidence and passed it—anonymously, of course—to the investigating officer, that would probably provide sufficient grounds for the investigators to get a federal search warrant."

"And how would the concerned citizen do that?"

Aleksy's gaze flickered. "He'd stick tight and hope for a break."

"Stick tight where?"

"He'd need to stay close by. Somewhere he could keep an eye on things."

He meant, stay in the cottage.

He meant, stay with her.

Faye felt as if she stood at the edge of a very large cliff. Her mouth was dry. Her hands were cold.

But instead of running for safety, she took another step toward the edge. "Then isn't it lucky I have a spare bedroom," she said.

"It's convenient." Aleksy grinned, and her pulse jumped for reasons that had nothing to do with fear. "Lucky would have been if I bunked in with you."

She inhaled sharply and almost choked on her wine.

When she was done coughing, Jarek murmured, "He's so damn tactful."

"That is why he gets all the girls," Eric called from the dining room.

Faye eased her grip on her wineglass. "All of them?"

Aleksy colored under his sunburn. "Hey, no, not all." He treated her to one of his charm-the-teacher grins and added, "Not yet."

Her heart lurched.

Jarek's eyes narrowed.

Tess reappeared in the doorway. "I must have missed something. I could have sworn you called your brother tactful."

"I was joking," Jarek explained. He looked at Faye, a mixture of sympathy and warning in his eyes. "Pop was kidding, too. Not about the number of women, though."

Aleksy raised both hands. "When you two are done assassinating my character, could we eat?"

"The paprikas is ready," Tess said.

"It smells wonderful," Faye said again, because it was true and she wanted to change the subject. She wasn't ready to jump off that particular cliff yet.

But as the meal progressed, she felt herself falling for the Denkos. All the Denkos.

Dinner was so much more than she was used to. More laughter. More arguments. More food. They talked constantly, over spilled milk and circulating dishes—chicken and mushrooms smothered in sour cream sauce, mashed potatoes with yellow pats of butter sliding down the sides, slivered cabbage and fragrant rye bread.

Mary was taking a rolled pastry covered in nuts and powdered sugar off the sideboard. Eric and Jarek, with Allie on his lap, debated the merits of spinners or minnows to catch some kind of fish. At the other end of the lace-covered cloth, Tess and Aleksy argued about the latest crime stats to come out of Chicago.

When Faye couldn't take another bite, when she was stuffed with food and drunk on noise, she grabbed the empty bread basket and headed for the kitchen. No one stopped her, no one jumped up and took the basket away and said, "Oh, no, let me." It made her feel part of it all, even as she fled.

Aleksy wandered in as she was arranging slices of bread. "Need a hand in here?"

She gave him a brilliant smile. "No, thanks. I've got it."

"Sure?"

"Yes." Because she was bursting out of her skin with feelings and paprikas, she blurted, "Thank you for inviting me."

He shrugged. "It's no big deal."

"It is for me," she said. "I live alone, remember?"

"Yeah, so do I."

"Yes, but this is your family."

"Ordinary family. Ordinary family dinner."

"Ordinary for you and Norman Rockwell, maybe."

He raised an eyebrow. "What, your family didn't have dinner?"

"Not like this." She ducked her chin to hide an old inadequacy. "I was an only child."

But he didn't let it go. "I thought you education types considered that an advantage? Both parents' full attention and all that."

"My parents divorced when I was four."

"Yeah?" Aleksy propped against the island and helped himself to a piece of bread. Something had sent Faye running for cover in the kitchen. He didn't intend to leave until he knew what it was. "That can be tough on a kid. Allie was about four when Jarek and her mom split."

Faye's brown eyes widened in distress. "Oh, I'm sorry."

He wasn't above using sympathy as an interview technique. But he hadn't counted on Faye's frustrating lack of self-regard. Whatever memories had shadowed her face a moment ago were forgotten in her instant concern for somebody else's kid. Where the hell were her personal boundaries? Where was her professional detachment?

"Hey, it was a while ago. She managed. Everybody manages, right?"

"I'm sure it helped that Allie has a father who cares about her," Faye said in her earnest teacher voice. "An uncle. Grandparents. Stepmother."

Bingo, he thought, watching her eyes. "Your mom never remarried?"

"Oh. Yes."

He waited. Nothing.

His gut tightened. His detective instincts stirred. After eight years on the force, he knew too much about the sick and sorry things that could go on in families to be easy with her brief response.

"Nice guy?" he persisted.

"Bob and Neil were both nice. I mean, neither of them had much time or interest in a child, but they were kind." She smiled faintly. "Neil remembered my birthday one year."

"Whoop-de-doo for Neil," he said, and enjoyed her stifled laugh. "How old were you?"

"Fourteen." Her hands stilled on the bread bag. Her eyes were far away. "He bought me flowers. Pink roses, and Mother was jealous."

Aleksy tried to think of the reasons Faye's mother could have to be jealous of her fourteen-year-old daughter. Tried not to think of them, as a quick, hard dread cramped his stomach. "What did she do?"

"Do?" Faye's lashes fluttered in confusion. "Well, she sent me to live with Aunt Eileen for a while."

The dread eased. "That sucks."

"Not really. I liked living with Aunt Eileen."

Okay, now he was pissed off. With her mother, for choosing her shiny new husband over her daughter.

With Faye, for accepting her fate.

With himself, for caring.

"That's no excuse for sending you away. She could have divorced the bastard."

"Well, she did, eventually." Faye pulled a wry face.

"I think she caught him sleeping with one of her graduate students."

"God. It's a wonder you're not more screwed up."

Oh, oops. Way to be a jerk, Denko. But it was too late to take it back.

And Faye, remarkably, was not offended. "Thank you. I think. I suppose I have my share of neuroses. Fortunately I also had Aunt Eileen."

"You were close?"

"She bought me my first paint set," Faye said simply. "Sometimes all it takes to make a difference in a child's life is one person to believe in them."

"An aunt," he said. It wasn't enough.

She smiled at him, and something snagged in his chest. "Or an uncle. I've seen you with Allie, remember."

He wouldn't be distracted. She had no idea what kind of guy he was, what made him tick. But he was beginning to get a very good idea of what drove her.

All it takes to make a difference in a child's life is one person to believe in them.

"Or a teacher," he guessed. "I bet you were a hell of a teacher."

Her smile faded. "I used to think so."

She looked so sad. Forlorn little pixie. To comfort her, to comfort them both, he leaned forward and dropped a kiss on her down-turned mouth.

Her lips parted in surprise. He felt the soft escape of her breath, saw the blood rise warm and irresistible under her baby-fine skin, watched her pupils dilate with desire and confusion.

And because he was a cop jerk bastard who took whatever was offered, he kissed her again.

Chapter 8

She tasted as sweet as the wine she'd been drinking and spicy as paprikas and, like the wine, she went to his head.

Her lips were full and soft and moist. Tasty. Aleksy traced them with his tongue. Nibbled them with his teeth. Faye hummed encouragement and curled her fingers in his shirt.

Hot damn, he thought, and then her tongue touched his and he didn't think at all. His mouth covered hers. Plundered hers. Again. His head was pounding. His heart was pounding. And she—it was the greatest thing—the cream puff art teacher kissed him back.

Her arms lifted to his shoulders. Her head fell back, in invitation or surrender, exposing the pale angle of her jaw and the fine veins just under her skin. He set his mouth to the tiny, wild pulse in her neck and heard her moan.

He dragged her against him, reveling in the feel of

her, all delicate bones and smooth skin and slight curves. So soft, so small. He devoured her mouth. So warm, so sweet.

So hot. He was burning up. His brain was on fire. He wanted her. Wanted to take her, hold her, have her, now.

He backed her against the island, and she lifted herself up on the countertop. Oh, yeah, that was good, even through the barrier of their clothes. He fit himself to her, heat to heat. The bread basket hit the floor. Her hands clutched his hair, and he—

"I suggest we have that talk." His brother's voice was hard and cold. It sluiced over Aleksy like rain in February. "Now."

Aleksy swore. Fiercely. Four letters.

"Not in my kitchen," Jarek said. "Not with our parents and my ten-year-old daughter on the other side of that door."

Faye gave a little moan and covered her face with both hands.

"Shut up," Aleksy snapped over his shoulder.

He turned his back on his brother, shielding Faye with his body. Circling her wrists gently with his fingers, he tugged to reveal her face. It was scarlet with humiliation. Her eyes were bright.

He cursed himself. He'd made her cry.

And then her gaze met his, and her lips curved in rueful amusement and he realized it wasn't tears shining in her eyes. It was laughter.

She thought this was funny?

She bit her lip, still erotically swollen from his kisses. "I'm sorry," she said. To him? To Jarek? "I came in for more bread."

Jarek's gaze flicked to the basket on the floor. "So I see."

Faye shifted her knees together, displacing Aleksy from between her thighs. "I, um—I guess I got distracted."

"I guess you did," Jarek agreed.

Aleksy bunched his shoulders, spoiling to take a swing at something, but his brother's tone was perfectly respectful. Admiring, even.

"Well." Faye hopped from the counter. "I'll just..." She dropped to her knees beside the scattered slices of rye. She began to dust them off, one by one, with her fingers and tuck them in the basket.

Some of Aleksy's resentment waned. She might be amused but at least she wasn't unaffected.

Wordlessly Jarek retrieved the bread bag from the counter and handed it to her.

"Oh." The color that had begun to retreat from her face flooded back. "Thank you."

Both men watched as she removed the slices that had been on the floor and replaced them with bread from the bag. By the time Aleksy figured out he could be helping her, she was already on her feet, clutching the basket.

"Got everything?" Jarek asked politely.

She looked at Aleksy. "Not yet."

Desire jolted through him. Her innuendo was completely unexpected. He wasn't sure his system could take any more surprises.

"Better get out there before they send in another search party," he said roughly.

She hesitated, as if she had something more to say. And then she nodded and left.

Aleksy braced his shoulders and faced his brother.

"What the *hell* were you thinking?" Jarek demanded.

"I wasn't thinking, okay?" Aleksy ran a hand through his hair. Because he knew Jarek was right, because he felt knocked off balance and guilty as a suspect with a smoking gun, he tried to shrug it off with a joke. "You know how it is when you eat one of Mom's meals. All your blood gets diverted from your brain to your stomach."

"Your blood was diverted, all right. And somewhere south of your stomach."

"Watch your mouth."

"What, you're insulted?"

"Not me." Aleksy struggled to explain feelings he didn't understand himself. "Just be careful what you say about her."

"Nice of you to be concerned. Too bad you weren't thinking about her before you backed her up against my kitchen counter."

"I only kissed her, for God's sake."

Although if Jarek hadn't walked in when he did...

"What do you want from her, Alex?" Jarek asked in his let's-be-reasonable voice. Rookies and criminals were sometimes tricked by that mild tone into relaxing their guard.

Aleksy knew better.

"What do you mean?"

"Do you want to sleep with her? Because if you do, I'd say you're making progress there. Or do you want to keep her safe? Because if you're starting to make headway on this case, then the best thing you can do for Faye Harper is to stay as far away from her as possible."

Good old Jare. You could always count on him to

take a two-horned dilemma and…run you right through the ribs with it.

"Am I?" Aleksy asked. "Making headway on the case?"

"I think so," said Jarek. "That Pilothouse in Toronto? The buyer was a Ziad Amir. He's with some international aid group headquartered there."

Adrenaline surged through Aleksy. He knew the name, if not the man. Before he was yanked from the case, he'd studied every file the feds had let him get his hands on.

"Yeah. Great organization. Providing aid to refugees and guns to terrorists," he said.

"Of course, we don't know for a fact the boat across the dock belongs to Amir," Jarek cautioned. "Or that he was visiting Freer. It could be a coincidence."

Aleksy paced. "Frickin' big coincidence."

This could be it. This could be the thread that led him to Karen's killers.

He stopped, brought up short by the realization of Faye's danger and the side of Jarek's refrigerator. "I have to get her out of that cottage."

"That might be difficult. Especially if the two of you are involved."

Aleksy shook his head. His blood supply might have relocated permanently to his groin, but some things didn't require much thought.

"Brother, you don't know me. The one thing I know is how to scare off a woman I'm involved with."

But Aleksy hadn't counted on the jolt of lust that zapped him when he walked out of the kitchen and saw Faye sitting beside Tess at the dining room table, her eyes lit with laughter and a tiny red smudge on her neck.

His mark on her skin.

He wasn't prepared for the admiration that crept through him when she acknowledged his presence without missing a beat of her conversation with his father.

He watched her teaching Allie to fold a stumpy origami swan out of a paper napkin and the tenderness that welled in him cut him off at the knees.

Scare her off? Of course he could.

But for the first time in his life, Aleksy thought he might regret seeing a woman go.

"And then you tuck it inside like this, see?" Faye reverse-folded a ninety degree angle in her napkin to form the neck of the swan, glad she had something to occupy her hands.

Every time she glanced at Aleksy her fingers tingled and her palms itched. And not for a pencil. Oh, she still longed to draw him, to try to capture his dark, sharp looks and all-male energy on paper. But Faye couldn't fool herself. Her appreciation of that hard, muscled chest and sculpted back wasn't strictly artistic anymore.

Seeing him with his family had blunted his edge, made him seem less dangerous. But not less desirable, she admitted to herself.

She envied his connections with his tight-knit family.

And she wanted to touch him again.

Faye creased the point of her napkin. "And you make the beak the same way," she said, keeping her hands and voice steady, demonstrating for Allie.

The girl squinted and nodded. "I get it. I got it!" She cried and waved her lopsided swan around.

"Very nice," said her grandmother.

"Let me see," Eric said.

Allie skipped from her seat. Faye smiled in pleasure, her gaze following the girl around the table until it smacked into Aleksy, standing by the oak breakfront.

The expression in his eyes melted her bones.

The phone rang.

Tess got up to answer it and reappeared a moment later, still holding the phone. "Jarek?"

He cupped his hand around the receiver and went into the kitchen. The conversations went on around the table, Eric admiring Allie's origami, Tess talking to Mary about doing a feature for the food section of the Eden Gazette and Faye trying to remember how to breathe.

She barely registered Jarek's return or his excuses.

"—have to go out for a little while."

Aleksy turned his head and something in the look the two brothers exchanged snapped Faye back to full attention. "Anything serious?"

"Domestic disturbance," Jarek said easily. "Nothing to worry about."

Eric frowned. "What kind of domestic disturbance call requires the chief of police on a Friday night?"

"We're a small department, Pop. I'm just providing cover for the responding officer." He bent to give Tess a brief, hard kiss. "Have coffee without me."

Faye had heard enough in the hallways and teachers' lounge to know that domestic violence often turned on those who tried to intervene.

Maybe Tess knew it, too, because her manicured nails pressed Jarek's sleeve. But all she said was, "I'll keep some hot."

As Jarek turned to go, Faye saw the black, snub shape of his gun at his waist. And her heart, which had been pattering along in pleased anticipation, gave a hard, uncomfortable bump.

How could Tess just let him go, without a warning or a protest?

Every time Jarek left this house, wearing that gun, he risked more than his life. He risked her heart.

Faye hated risk.

Aleksy said something that made Mary Denko laugh, and Allie walked her father to the front door.

Faye stayed where she was while a new fear uncurled in her stomach. Getting involved with Aleksy could be dangerous in ways she had never imagined.

Aleksy glanced at the passenger side of the TransAm. Faye sat with her face turned to the window and her wrist cradled in her lap. Since leaving his brother's house, she had barely looked at him, had hardly spoken.

Obviously he wasn't going to have to work very hard at scaring her off. Somebody or something had already done it for him.

The thought brought him no satisfaction at all.

Since the mood was ruined anyway, he figured he couldn't make things worse. Might as well pass on to her the latest bad news from home.

"I made a call before dinner," he told her. "On that kid of yours."

Her eyes widened. "Jamal?"

"Yeah. I've got a buddy who works juvie over in Area 2. I asked him to do some checking, run his name through the system."

"I told you I didn't want your help."

Okay. Fine.

"Suit yourself," he said.

Tight-lipped, he let the car out a little on the straightaway. He was almost in the mood to be pulled over by some self-important Smokey with too much time on his hands.

"Did he—did you learn anything?" Faye asked over the roar of the engine.

The hope and worry packed in that one tight question twisted something inside him. He eased up on the accelerator.

"It's not good," he warned.

"Tell me."

Right, he thought. She asked for it. And maybe telling her would remind her of the dangers of getting emotionally involved with anyone.

"He's definitely using. Two weeks ago, he was picked up and charged with possession of crank. That's methamphetamine," he explained.

"I know what crank is."

Well, yeah, teaching at Lincoln, she would.

"His court date's been set for the twenty-third," Aleksy continued. "A good lawyer could make the case that he was holding less than fifteen grams, he's under eighteen and it's a first offense. That's the good news. He can't be convicted to more than a year in prison and he could get off with a fine."

"That's good news?"

From Aleksy's perspective, a cop's perspective, the kid was getting off lightly. But he supposed that Faye, as a bleeding heart teacher, might see things differently.

"You're breaking your heart over nothing, you know."

She raised her pointy little chin. "Excuse me?"

He merged easily with the cars heading north around the lake. Weekend traffic, trying to get a jump on a few more hours of summer fun before Monday morning's rat race. "Kids like that—at-risk kids—slip through the cracks all the time. There isn't anything you can do about it."

"Oh, and so I shouldn't try?"

The light of battle in her eyes baffled him. She was the one suffering from burnout, wasn't she?

"Sure, you can try. But at some point you've got to accept that, as a teacher, the odds are against you."

"The odds are against you as a law enforcement officer, too." She lifted one eyebrow. "Or do you imagine that you can single-handedly wipe out crime in Chicago?"

Damn, she was slippery. And smart.

"All I'm saying is, you can't do your job if you let yourself care too much," he said stubbornly.

"What if you don't care enough? Can you do it then?"

Aleksy set his jaw. "Okay, so you care. Some. But you set limits. You can't make it personal."

"So, it's never personal for you?"

Hell. She was too damn close to busting him open. In another minute she'd remember what he'd told her about Karen and start grilling him about his reasons for being here.

"Never," he lied.

"I don't believe you."

He jerked one shoulder. "Believe what you want."

"I think you only asked your friend to investigate Jamal because you cared about me."

Huh?

He slowed the car so he could look at her. The light of the setting sun slanted through the windshield. Faye's eyes were soft and glowing.

"I'm not saying I like what you found out but I appreciate that you were trying to help." She leaned across the console and brushed warm lips against his cheek. "Thank you."

He was so screwed.

Aleksy flung a rock over the wide, dark water. He heard it skip once, twice, three times before it sank like a—well, like a stone.

God, it was quiet out here. And dark. He missed Chicago's streetlights, the blare of traffic, the roar of the elevated train. But here he was, with the frogs and the fish and the lapping lake, trying to put some distance between himself and the quiet sounds of Faye preparing for bed.

He looked out at the pulsing stars and whispering water, separated by a black band of trees and shore. He could see the occasional yellow gleam of a window and, across the lake, Freer's security lights illuminating an empty triangle of grass.

A good detective operated by asking the questions that would help him develop a plan of action. Aleksy had questions, all right. He just didn't have a damn plan.

How the hell was he supposed to scare Faye off when she persisted in seeing him as some kind of good guy?

The screen door scraped open behind him. He tensed as he heard soft footsteps cross the deck. Swell. She was coming out. The last thing either of them needed right now was a romantic tryst by moonlight. He shoved his hands in his pockets.

Although... Hey. Maybe that was the solution. Faye had already made it clear she wasn't ready for a relationship. Maybe he should pull her down on the rough dock and demonstrate some of the reasons she ought to be afraid of him. It could work. He would get to touch her again and she could slap his face.

He hunched his shoulders, staring out over the water. Yeah, and if she didn't? If she cried or, worse, cooperated? What would he do if she opened her arms to him the way she had in his brother's kitchen? If she opened those warm, soft lips? If she opened—

He was sweating, though the air was cool enough now to warrant a jacket. If Faye didn't stop him, did he really trust himself to call a halt to things?

She didn't make a sound crossing the muddy lawn but he knew when she stepped on the dock. With a cop's sixth sense, with a lover's awareness, he felt her come up behind him.

"You should go in," he said roughly.

Yeah, that was good. He sounded like one tough son of a bitch.

She didn't buy it. "Why?"

He took a deep, annoyed breath. "Are you trying to start something? Or do you truly not get it?"

Something pale moved in the shadows at the corner of his eye. She didn't touch him, but neither did she run. He saw the flutter of her skirt as she sat down at the edge of the dock.

"What is it that I'm not getting?" she asked. A hint of mischief infected her tone and started a fever in his blood. "Besides sex, I mean?"

"You can't stay here," he said desperately. She had taken off her sandals and was dangling her pretty, narrow, naked feet above the water. "It's dangerous."

"No one's going to attack me sitting at the end of my aunt's dock at nine o'clock at night," she said reasonably.

"I might," he muttered.

She laughed, low and sleepy like the bird's call.

He swore. This was it. He was going to have to tell her—a civilian, a woman—the truth.

Not the whole truth, he reassured himself. But enough to convince her to go running back to Chicago.

"Faye, listen. Jarek told me tonight he found a connection between the boat you drew and the men I'm after."

"That's what you expected, isn't it? That's what you wanted."

"Yeah. The thing is, now that we know—" he didn't really know, not without the registration number, but that was one piece of evidence he was holding back "—you need to rethink seriously about staying here. These guys aren't amateurs. You don't want to mess with them."

No, she didn't. But she said, "I am not going back to Chicago. Besides, if they thought I was a threat, they would have done more than simply break into my house to steal some photographs and a painting."

"You were lucky."

"You mean, because I scared them off? You think they would have taken more?"

"Sweetheart, they got everything they came for. You were lucky they didn't kill you."

She shivered. "Oh."

"Yeah. 'Oh.' I don't want anything to happen to you, damn it." The words burst out of him. "I feel guilty enough already."

Faye stilled her feet in the cool, swirling water.

Guilt, she understood. But it wasn't a motivation she expected to have in common with Detective Don't-Take-It-Personally Denko.

"Guilty about what?" she asked softly.

He was silent so long she thought he wasn't going to answer her.

"I already have to live with one woman's death on my conscience," he said finally, harshly. "I don't want to live with yours."

Her skin prickled. If he was trying to frighten her, he was doing a good job. Yet the pain in his voice tugged at her. Silhouetted against the stars, his shoulders were rigid. His sharp profile was bleak and alone.

Because it hurt her heart to look at him, she spoke briskly, as if she were talking to one of her students. "Don't you think you're taking this guilt trip a little too far? It's not like you're Blue Beard or something."

He turned his head to look at her. "Who?"

"Blue Beard. You know, the man who murdered all his wives and locked their bodies in a tower?"

Aleksy continued to stare. "You mean, like Gacy? With the boys under the floorboards?"

Faye felt her face warm in the dark. "Well, sort of. Blue Beard is a character. In a fairy tale."

"This isn't some fairy tale. I'm not Prince Charming, and there is no happily ever after. This is the real world, sweetheart, and in the real world, sometimes the wrong people die."

She heard his temper and it started her own, a quick, hot lick of it along her nerves. But she heard his pain, too. "Don't condescend to me, Aleksy. I know all about the real world. I taught for four years in a real high school."

"Right," he said tightly. "Sorry. Then—"

She swung her feet out of the water and dried them on her skirt. "And your version of reality is as big a fantasy as any bedtime story I ever heard."

"What the hell are you talking about?"

Her heart hammered so hard she thought she might be sick. She took a deep breath to steady her nerves and her stomach. "You weren't even there when your partner—former partner—was killed. How can you be guilty of her death?"

He yanked her to her feet. His hands gripped her shoulders. His breath was ragged against her face. "Because I *wasn't* there, damn it. Because if I hadn't screwed things up, Karen wouldn't have put in for a transfer. She would never have been assigned to that case. I'm responsible."

"*She* put in for the transfer," Faye repeated, willing him to hear her. "*She* accepted the case. What happened was awful, yes, it was wrong, maybe it could have been prevented, I don't know. But it wasn't your fault. Her choices were her responsibility."

"And you believe that?" Aleksy challenged her.

Faye raised her chin, which still left it at the level of his chest. "Why wouldn't I?"

"I'm just trying to figure how you get to be responsible for your students, but I'm not responsible for my partner."

She stared at him, stunned from the quick, dirty blow. He was a cop, she reminded herself. He was trained in street-fighting and self-defense.

"Well, the situations are different, aren't they?"

"Are they?"

"Yes. You said it yourself. Jamal is still a student. A child. Karen was an adult woman. A police officer." Faye's voice gained in confidence. "She knew the risks. She chose to take them."

"So, according to your theory, as long as she went into things with her eyes open, I'm off the hook."

It was hard to think with his hands bruising her shoulders, with his gaze boring into hers. It was hard to breathe. The starlight gave a primitive cast to his face. Heat, tension, anger poured off of him in waves.

She wet her lips with her tongue. Whispered, ''Yes.''

His grip shifted. His eyes blazed. ''Then open your eyes, cream puff. Because I'm about to make my move.''

Chapter 9

She expected him to jerk. She was braced for him to grab. But Aleksy did exactly as he had warned, giving her time to change her mind, giving her a chance to pull away. One hand slid to circle her throat. The other traced her ribs, skimmed her back, lightly.

Her pulse went wild under the rough pad of his fingers. Keeping his eyes on hers, he lowered his head, blotting out the lake and the night behind him. She felt the slow rise of heat, from him, in her. His sharp features blurred.

And he stopped, a breath from her lips.

He was leaving her the choice, Faye realized. He was handing her the responsibility.

The idea should have terrified her. Did terrify her. She laid a hand on his chest. His heart slammed against her palm.

An adult woman knew the risks. It was up to her whether she chose to take them.

Faye's fingers flexed. Her mouth curved. "Kiss me or die, Detective."

A sound exploded from him, part laugh, part groan, and the hand on her back tightened as the hand on her throat slipped up into her hair. He brought her closer—*not close enough*—and finally he kissed her, his mouth hot and moving on hers. She fisted her hand in his shirt to hold him to her, to hold herself up.

He tasted wonderful, dark and intense. She caught her breath with pleasure and the risk she was taking. Again, they kissed, slow, exploring kisses, wet, deep kisses, like a couple of high school students plastered against the lockers between classes, completely absorbed in and needing only each other. Except none of her students had a body like his, heavy with muscle, honed with experience. She rubbed against him, trying to absorb more sensation, and his arousal ground against her.

Faye shivered, relieved and nervous at the same time. *You like me*, she thought with an inner giggle. *You really like me.*

He wrapped her closer. "Cold?"

She blinked at him. Was she cold? She did a quick inventory. Her arms were okay. Her long skirt protected her legs.

"Just my feet." They were bare, and still damp.

"Well, we can't have you getting cold feet at this point." His voice was husky and amused.

He scooped her up—she clutched him in surprise—and sat down on the dock, with her sideways in his lap.

"What are you doing?"

He reached for her legs, drawing them up beside his thigh. "Warming your feet."

"You're kidding."

"Nope."

She started to straighten her legs. "It will tickle."

He held her fast, one arm behind her back, the other wrapping her knees. "Not if I do it right."

Ignoring her wiggling, he began to massage her feet with one strong, lean hand. It felt strange. Good. A restless yearning uncurled in her stomach and traveled along her limbs as he pressed and kneaded her arch, rotated her ankles, pushed his finger between her toes. She moaned and he laughed.

"You're very good," she accused.

"Practice," he explained.

She didn't doubt it.

She didn't want to think about it. Not when what he was doing felt so good.

He worked his way past her ankles and up her calves, stroking and rubbing. She felt her thighs loosen, her knees part. He took advantage of the opening, his warm, rough hand sliding along her inner thigh, massaging the muscles there.

Her head lolled back against his shoulder. She closed her eyes, seduced by the magic of his touch and the musky smell of his skin. Her nipples tightened. His breath rasped as he worked her, under her skirt, gliding up, pressing down.

Just a little farther, she urged him in her mind. She squirmed in his lap. *Up. There.*

His touch was firm and hot. He moved slower. Higher. She trembled. When he finally touched her *there,* she was wet and ready for him.

He grunted in satisfaction. His hand, blunt and seeking, slid up over her belly and down into her underwear. She arched against his fingers, squirmed in his lap.

He pulled his hand away.

No, no, no.

She grabbed at his shoulders, nipped at his lower lip.

"Easy," he said. "I just want to—"

She fused her mouth to his.

Heat erupted from him. Poured into her. This time, his kiss was hard and hungry and a little mean. A thrill chased through her as he shifted and rolled her until she was flat on her back on the dock. He tugged at her hem so that she lay on the back of her skirt and positioned himself between her legs.

"I'll probably get splinters in my knees," he grumbled.

She laughed up at him, feeling reckless and unafraid. "I don't care."

His grin flashed in the dark. "Hell, neither do I."

He yanked down her panties and spread her thighs. Her heart hammered.

"Wait," she said.

He froze above her. "You're joking."

An adult woman knew the risks and took responsibility.

"Condoms," she said. "Do you have any?"

"Oh. Yeah. In my wallet."

Well, that was good. Wasn't it? He was prepared.

Her mind flashed back to the afternoon, to Tess's cheerful inquiry. *So, how do you like living with the Boy Scout?*

She stared up at the night sky while Aleksy stripped off his pants and fumbled in the pocket. Good idea? Bad idea? Did she really know what she was doing? Did she really know him well enough to—

He pinned her against the dock, taking most of his weight on his elbows. His body was hard and lean. His arousal was blunt and hot. Her mind shied, but her hips lifted.

He kissed her and then drew back. "You're getting cold feet again," he observed.

She was embarrassed. How could he tell? "Maybe. A little."

He shifted on top of her. Rocked against her. "Guess I'll have to warm you up, then."

Warm. Yes. She felt the roughness of his thighs, the smoothness of his sex, and her own muscles softened and loosened in response.

"We could go inside," she suggested.

"Inside," he repeated reflectively and rocked again, harder, higher up.

Her lungs emptied. "Yes," she said.

He reached between their bodies, positioning himself, parting her. Oh, yes.

"I'd like to be inside," he whispered, stroking. "Take me inside, sweetheart."

When he put it that way, when he touched her that way, how could she resist? He nuzzled her neck.

Anyway, she was tired of resisting, tired of living in shades of gray. She wanted raw and vivid and warm and wonderful. She wanted sex on a dock under a brilliant night sky and Aleksy. She shuddered with her own daring. And he must have read that as encouragement, because he thrust inside her then, thick and solid, real and male, slick and stunning.

Her mouth opened. Oh.

Aleksy's hand tightened in her hair until she looked at him, dazed. "Like that," he said. "Just like that."

He moved over her and in her, deeper, faster, building a rhythm that made her heart race. She clutched at his shoulders, pressed her feet flat against the dock. She could hear the lap of the water and the slap of flesh on flesh, and her own short, explosive breaths as he came into her, plunged into her, again and again. His face was fierce and unfocused. The stars whirled behind his head. Dizzied, she clung to him, until the night sky streaked down in color like a paint box left in the rain, and she fell off the edge of the world.

She heard his shout as he tumbled after her.

Aleksy was good at exits.

He had perfected I-have-to-get-up-early-it-was-wonderful-I'll-call-you, right down to the last warm squeeze and significant look at the door.

A good exit kept things from getting messy. Kept people from getting hurt.

He paced the length of the braided rug. It was harder, he was discovering, when you had to stick around.

It was a damn sight harder when the woman was Faye.

He heard her turn off the shower in the next room and pictured her wet and naked, reaching for one of those fluffy green towels. He still hadn't seen her without all her clothes, but he knew the shape of her breasts now, the slope of her hips, the curve of her tight little butt. He'd learned the smell of her soap and the texture of her skin.

He stared out at the black lake, his jaw tense and his imagination running wild. When they had staggered back to the cottage, she'd invited him to shower with her, her face a pretty pink.

What if he'd said yes? What if he went in there right now and—

Bad idea.

One of a string of bad ideas, starting with "let me stay with you."

His brother was right. Aleksy needed to separate the

personal and professional areas of his life before somebody got hurt.

He heard Faye humming and winced. Too late. His knees already stung. His conscience smarted. And Faye, warm, sweet Faye, with her wounded idealism and her unexpected passion, was a five-car pileup waiting to happen.

She wandered into the living room, wearing a sleeveless cotton dress that swirled around her calves and showed the outline of her nipples. Her short damp hair glistened like gold. Her feet were bare.

He went hard as rock.

She smiled at him. "Bathroom's all yours."

He fisted his hands at his sides. "Thanks."

The smile faded. "What's wrong?"

"Nothing."

Nothing except every time he looked at her he wanted to back her against the nearest available surface and take her again.

Her brows drew together. Concern shone in her eyes. Crossing the room—*don't look at her breasts*—she touched his arm with warm, light fingers.

"Do you want to talk about it?"

Panic stirred. This is how it started. They always wanted to talk.

He sighed. "Yeah. Maybe we better."

He took her hand—she had really great hands, the kind you'd expect an artist to have, long fingered and smooth. The memory of those hands on his body made him break out in a sweat—anyway, he took her hand and sat on the couch with her.

"The thing is—" he started.

She looked at him expectantly.

And his quick-thinking brain went blank. His fast-talking mouth went dry.

"The thing is," she prompted.

"I really like you," he said.

She drew her hand away. "If this is the part where you tell me you want us always to be friends, someone is going to get hurt."

That was exactly what he was trying to prevent.

"No. I don't want us to be friends. I mean, friends, fine, sure, but—I *really* like you, Faye."

Her slim shoulders relaxed a little.

"I want us to see each other," he continued. "When we get back to Chicago."

Her lips curved. "That's planning ahead."

To the end of the summer, she meant. She thought he would still want to see her, sleep with her, three months from now.

Aleksy waited for the spurt of discomfort, of denial, and was astonished when it didn't come.

"Yeah. The thing is—" He cleared his throat. "I think you should go back to Chicago now."

Her eyes narrowed. "Excuse me?"

"You're in danger here. I think you should leave. At least until I get the proof I need and things settle down."

She shook her head. "We already talked about this. I told you I accepted the risks. Nothing has changed."

He felt a lance of fear, sharp and unfamiliar. He covered it with irritation. "What do you mean, nothing has changed? We're sleeping together."

"We haven't slept together," she said. "You couldn't roll off me fast enough. We had sex."

"Great sex."

Her lips pressed together. "It must have been really

special for you to be in this big a hurry to get rid of me.''

He was genuinely appalled. ''You can't think that!''

''What else should I think?''

''You could think maybe I care about you,'' he snapped. ''Maybe I don't want to have to worry about you.''

''Well, isn't that too bad.'' She stood. ''I, of course, wouldn't need to worry about you if I went running off to Chicago and left you here in the middle of God knows what kind of danger. Where did you plan on staying?''

He hadn't planned. She was wrecking his thought processes. ''I hoped you'd let me stay here.''

''In my aunt's cottage,'' she said flatly.

He shrugged. ''I can pay rent, if you want.''

''That's not the point. The point is, you've already made sure the whole town thinks you're my boyfriend.''

She was concerned about his cover. She was trying to protect him. He was touched.

''It's okay,'' he assured her. ''I'll make something up. Pretend we had a fight or something.''

''You don't have to pretend.'' Her voice was clear and sharp as glass. ''We are having a fight. And I am not leaving.''

Faye dragged a broad, wet brush across the top of her page, blending blue and purple to create a peaceful cloud layer in a soothing sky.

Okay, so she wasn't feeling that peaceful, she admitted to herself. The edge of her brush had caught some unfortunate cadmium red, and she hated painting at night.

But she couldn't sleep. She refused to cry. And she

would teach watercoloring to the wrestling team before she would run away again.

She stepped back, barefoot, to squint at her painting. No, this time Detective Hit-and-Run Denko was the one beating a retreat.

I really like you, Faye.

Ha.

She streaked an angry orange line across the horizon. Sunset, she decided, approving the way it punched up the red, and dug her brush into the raw sienna for good measure. Take that, paper.

She was a grown woman. She was a grown artist. She could paint outside the lines if she wanted. She could live outside the box.

Until Aleksy got tired of playing with her and put her away again.

The rat.

Her brush shook. The sky blurred. She blinked fiercely.

Okay, so she'd just bared her soul and gotten naked on a dock with a man who wanted to keep her safely under wraps. That didn't mean she had to accept his restrictions.

Did she?

Aleksy winced. He was sitting on the couch with his pants around his ankles, picking splinters from his knees.

If he needed any proof he was too damn old to screw on a dock, this was it.

The thought depressed him.

He wasn't that old. He pinched the skin around the splinter, forcing it to the surface. Just old enough to start taking precautions. He should have supplied a blanket.

And he should never, ever have put the moves on a woman he couldn't walk away from, a woman he could care about.

Not that he'd get the chance to now. The splinter resisted his fingers. The only woman he cared about was barely speaking to him. He didn't figure she'd invite him to inspect the planks at the end of her dock anytime soon.

His knees were safe. His bachelor lifestyle was protected.

So, how come he still felt lousy?

Aleksy sighed and poked at the splinter with the tip of his pocket knife.

Faye stopped dead in the living room door. "What are you doing?"

He stabbed at his knee and swore. "What does it look like?"

"It looks like you need to pull up your pants," she said primly, but she took a step forward.

His body twitched. He did his best to ignore it. "Yeah, well, I was in my room but the light's better out here."

"Better for what? Oh." A wave of pink washed from her throat to the tips of her pretty ears. "You have a splinter."

"Splinters," he said grimly. "And I'm dealing with them."

Her brows arched. "With a knife? You're supposed to use a needle."

"Gee. Guess I left my sewing kit at home," he drawled.

Silenced, she stood and watched his clumsy attempts to pry bits of wood from beneath his skin. His palms dampened. The bulge in his boxers grew. He didn't

know whether to be sorry or relieved when she finally
pivoted and left him.

He sucked in his breath. He almost had this sucker.
He pinched the protruding end of the splinter with his
fingernails and…broke it off beneath the skin.

"Damn."

"Oh, here," Faye said impatiently. "Let me."

She was back, wearing that long blue dress that
cupped her breasts and left her arms bare. She had a
needle and tweezers in her grasp and a determined look
in her eyes.

Hell, he wasn't getting anywhere. Let her see what
she could do.

He leaned back against the cushions of the couch.
Would she notice he was already half aroused?

"Be my guest," he said.

Her throat moved as she swallowed. But she knelt
bravely on the floor between his legs, resting one hand
on his hairy thigh for balance. Beneath his boxers, his
body strained for her attention.

Faye kept her head demurely lowered. Her gaze fixed
on his knee. Her hands trembled slightly.

She was going to kill him, he thought, resigned. But
it would be worth it.

She touched his knee, her fingers warm and light.

He closed his eyes. *Just a little higher, sweetheart.*

Her needle probed under his skin. Before he could
do more than draw a breath, she extracted the splinter.

"That's one," she said, holding it up for his inspection.

He exhaled. "Great."

"I'm not done," she warned.

Even better.

Her slight weight leaned against his leg. Her elbow

rested on his thigh. Aleksy sniffed. If he let himself lean forward, her flower-scented hair would brush his chin. He felt himself swell at the thought.

He spread his arms along the back of the couch. "Do your worst. I'm in your hands."

She frowned. Hesitated. Jabbed.

He sat up fast. "Ouch."

"Oh, I'm so sorry."

She sounded flustered. Mortified.

Maybe she was mad at him, but she was too soft-hearted to willingly hurt anybody. Cream puff, he thought.

He studied her. Despite her wild blush, her face was drawn. Fatigue pulled at the corners of her mouth and bruised the delicate skin under her eyes. Tenderness tugged at him.

"You look tired," he observed.

She shot him an annoyed look. "Thank you. I'm fine."

"You sleep all right?"

"No." She pressed the tweezers to his skin. "I stayed up too late."

He felt a spurt of purely male gratification. At least he wasn't the only one suffering.

"We must have had the same dream," he said.

Her eyes gleamed. She extracted another splinter. "I doubt it. I was working."

"Ouch," he said again.

She bent her head, but not before he saw her smile.

He grinned like a fool. She wasn't as immune as she liked to pretend.

She had the prettiest neck. He wondered what she'd do if he brushed aside those soft, pale tendrils of hair and kissed the delicate skin of her throat. Probably stick him with her needle.

To distract himself, he asked, "So, what were you working on?"

She nodded toward the magnet strip board propped against her worktable. "It's over there. This one's going to hurt," she cautioned.

He sucked in his breath and glanced toward the table as she drew another splinter from his abraded knee.

Well.

Wow.

"That's different," he said.

She glared at him. "Different, how?"

"It's—" Jeez, how was he supposed to describe what he was seeing? It was a landscape, kind of, but the whole thing throbbed with color and pulsed with life. Fierce reds contended with angry purples in a violent sky. The hills smoked. The water steamed. "It's red."

She sat back on her heels. "I've used red before."

"Not like that." He didn't know anything about art, but he was certain he hadn't seen anything like this before.

"You hate it."

"No," he said. "No, I guess I'm trying to decide if I had a narrow escape last night or missed something really hot."

Faye gaped at him, flattered. Shaken. Confused. *Art should evoke an emotional response,* she'd told him. Did he remember? He had a good memory. Would he use it against her?

Abruptly, she pushed to her feet, using his warm, muscled thigh for support, and scrambled back. "You're done."

"Okay." He stood slowly. He hitched his jeans over his lean hips and—well, over everything. With some difficulty, he zipped his fly. Her face flamed.

"Thanks," he said. "Your turn."

"Excuse me?"

"You just picked enough wood out of my knees to build a bookshelf. The least I can do is return the favor."

She had told herself she would not run again.

She'd lied.

"My knees are fine," she said.

"Sure?"

"Yes."

"Maybe I should check for you. You did spend a lot of time on your—" he paused wickedly "—back."

Her insides went warm gold as she remembered the stars pulsing behind his head and him pulsing inside her.

Could she take what he was offering and still hide her feelings from him? Could she hide them from herself?

She straightened her spine before she melted in a little puddle at his feet. "Thanks, but no thanks."

He took a step closer, hot, dark and dangerous. Her breath hitched.

"I don't mind playing doctor," he said, his voice husky.

"That's too bad," she said. Could he hear her heart? It was beating so hard she was shaking with it. "Because I don't want to play with you."

Although, heaven help her, when she was kneeling between his thighs a minute ago, she'd certainly thought about it.

Aleksy scowled. "Okay. No games. Faye, I—"

And someone knocked on the front door.

Chapter 10

"I'll get it."

In a smooth move that looked borrowed from a police drama, Aleksy flowed toward the door.

Faye's mouth went dry. Her hormones signaled that this was prime alpha male stuff and she should start making babies with it immediately.

"I can get the door," she said more sharply than she intended. "This is my house."

He frowned. "Are you expecting anybody?"

"No." She marched past him into the dark hallway. "Are you?"

The shadow behind the screen—big, black and rangy—made her check her stride. And then her visitor stepped back into the sunlight, and she recognized his black-and-orange football jersey and close-cropped head.

Joy coursed through her, surging through her guilt, rushing past her doubts.

"Jamal!" She flew to unlock the screen.

The seventeen-year-old jerked his chin in greeting. "Hey, Harp." Super casual. Super cool.

But when she grabbed him in a hug, one arm lifted and patted her back awkwardly.

She gripped his jersey—the Bear's Urlacher 54—and held him at arm's length to get a better look. "What are you doing here?"

"My stepdad threw me out."

With dismay, she saw the worn book bag at his feet, its seams strained to bursting. "Oh, Jamal. Why?"

He shifted his feet. "He got mad about some sh— something and told me to get out." The boy shrugged. "So I did."

"Was it your arrest?" Faye asked.

Jamal's eyes widened. "You know about that?"

"She knows," Aleksy said behind her. "You want to keep your bad habits to yourself, you shouldn't hang out on street corners with associates who are known to the police."

The boy jerked. "Who the hell is he?"

"A friend," Faye said, although at the moment she could have strangled him. "Jamal King, Aleksy Denko."

"*Detective* Denko," Aleksy said.

"Right." Jamal's tone flattened with betrayal. "See you around, Harp."

Faye kept tight hold of his shirt. "Don't you dare leave. You have to at least come in for—" what? she thought frantically "—something to drink."

His dark, wary eyes flicked to the man behind her. "I don't know, Miz Harper, I—"

But she tugged him through the door, using her slight weight and a stream of conversation to nudge him toward the living room. Aleksy moved silently out of their way.

"Why, you're sweating," Faye said. "What did you do, walk from Chicago?"

Jamal adjusted his grip on his book bag. His hands shook slightly. "I took the train to, what is it, Eden. Walked from there."

"That must be five miles. No wonder you look hot."

"He looks high," Aleksy said.

Faye's heart clutched. He did. Oh, he did.

"Sit here," she told Jamal, practically pushing him onto the couch. "I'll get you a soda. Aleksy, could I speak with you in the kitchen?"

He stalked behind her. "What?" he demanded as she closed the kitchen door.

"I don't want you saying things like that in front of Jamal."

"Like what? Like, he's high? Take a good look, sweetheart. Shaky hands, rapid breathing, the sweats…"

"It's the visit. He's nervous."

"It's the drugs. He's belligerent, too."

She raised her eyebrows. "Is that any wonder, with the way you're treating him?"

Aleksy paced the short length of the kitchen. "What about the dilated pupils?"

She'd noticed Jamal's eyes, too. She sighed. "All right, I know he may be using. But—"

"No 'maybe' about it."

"Just give me a chance to talk to him."

Aleksy thrust his hands in his pockets. "You'll have to talk to Family Services, too."

"I am not reporting that child to the Department of Family Services!"

"Not him." Aleksy's voice was suddenly serious. Quiet. "The stepfather. If the parents kicked the kid out, they could be guilty of neglect."

"But...he's seventeen."

"Statute covers children up to eighteen years old. As a school employee, you're obliged to report suspected cases of neglect. Or the court could find you guilty of a Class A misdemeanor."

She pressed her fingers to her eyeballs. "Oh, God."

Hard and sure, his arms came around her. She stiffened and then let herself lean on him, absorbing the thud of his heart and his unexpected comfort.

"Call the department," he urged. "Let them sort it out. They have the resources to help a kid like that. You don't need to get involved."

"That's what I told myself when I came here. Crawled here," she corrected wryly, "to lick my wounds. Don't get involved. Don't get hurt."

Aleksy's arms tightened around her. "It's good advice."

She shook her head against his shoulder. "It didn't work with you."

"I'm not going to hurt you."

She lifted her head to meet his gaze. "Aren't you?"

Color moved across his cheekbones under his faint tan. "I don't want to hurt you. And I don't want anybody else hurting you, either."

"Jamal needs my help."

His arms fell away. "He needs detox. And family counseling."

She tried not to mind the loss of his embrace. "And do you really think he's going to get either one if he leaves here?"

"He can't stay. He's a speed freak, for God's sake. He could have hallucinations. He could turn violent."

She was shaken. But she refused to be discouraged. "He's not that far gone."

"How would you know? You haven't seen him in weeks."

She bit her lip. "I guess we'll have to see how he does and deal with any behavioral problems as they arise."

"Damn it, Faye, I've got better things to do with my time than baby-sit the 'behavioral problems' of a seventeen-year-old junkie."

Familiar guilt stirred, and unfamiliar temper.

She spoke carefully. "I'm sorry if Jamal's presence hampers your investigation."

"It's not only the case." Aleksy took another frustrated circuit of the room. "You have to admit having him here complicates things."

Oh, yes, that was temper hissing under her skin. It forced her to turn and face him. To face what she was to him. And what she wanted to be.

"What things?" Faye asked.

He turned and looked at her. "Things. Us."

"You mean sex," she said flatly. "You mean it might be difficult for two unattached adults to have sex with a sick child staying in the same small house."

Hell.

Aleksy glared at her with equal parts anger and admiration. She made an unlikely warrior, this pixie art teacher armed with nothing more formidable than big brown eyes and good intentions. But she'd stabbed him that time.

"I'm just pointing out that you already have a lot to deal with right now."

She raised her chin. "Then I'll deal with it. Excuse me." She brushed by him on her way to the refrigerator. "I promised Jamal I'd get him a Coke."

Aleksy's jaw set. If he couldn't scare Faye, then by God he would intimidate the kid.

He tailed her to the living room and propped against the mantel, crossing his arms against his chest and looking mean.

Faye ignored his badass routine. Crossing the room, she touched the boy gently on the shoulder. "Jamal? I've got your soda."

He twitched. "Huh? Oh. Thanks."

His hands were locked between his knees—to stop their trembling, Aleksy judged. The kid freed one to accept the glass. He took two sips and set it aside.

His dark, dilated gaze fixed on Faye with painful hope. He didn't look at Aleksy at all. "You sure it's okay? Me coming here like this?"

She sat on the couch beside him, stilling his hands between both her own. "I'm glad you came," she said firmly. "But we need to talk about whether you can stay."

"I got no place else to go," the boy said. "I told you. Ron threw me out."

"Your mother have anything to say about that?" Aleksy asked from his post by the fireplace.

One shoulder jerked. "She pretty much says what Ron tells her to."

It happened. It happened all the time. Aleksy tried not to care. "Did you know if a teacher suspects a student is being neglected or abused, she has a legal obligation to report her suspicions to the authorities?"

Faye stirred against the cushions of the couch. "This isn't the time—"

"So?" said the kid.

Aleksy hardened his voice and his heart. "So, do you want Miss Harper to report your parents? Or would you prefer she got in trouble with the law?"

Faye stood, her slim form almost vibrating with fury. "Okay, that's enough. Why don't you go do your job or something?"

"I am doing my job," Aleksy said doggedly. "I'm protecting you." He turned back on the teen. "Well? Is that what you want?"

Faye's eyes narrowed dangerously. "I said—"

"No!" The word burst from the boy. He lurched to his feet. "I didn't mean— I didn't want— Ron didn't really throw me out. I just said that so you'd have to take me in."

Score one for the big, bad detective. Except that the kid's confession didn't make Aleksy feel any better. And it didn't seem to have any effect on Faye at all.

"All right," she soothed. "All right."

She put her slim arm around the boy's big shoulders and urged him to sit. It should have looked funny, the tiny blond woman trying to mother the hyped-up, overgrown punk, but a hard, hot lump in Aleksy's throat stopped him from laughing.

"Do they know where you are?" Faye asked softly.

"No." The kid's shoulders hunched. "We did have a fight. I didn't make that part up. Ron was yelling and stuff. Well, you know how he is."

Faye's hand crept to massage her wrist and Aleksy's gut clenched.

"Yes," she said. "I know."

"So I got out before he did something I would have

had to—'' The boy's gaze slid to Aleksy. ''Anyway, I got out.''

Aleksy uncrossed his arms. ''Is there someone you can stay with until your stepfather cools down?''

Faye's face took on a confused, indignant look, like a cab passenger discovering his driver spoke only Farsi. ''Me,'' she insisted. ''He can stay with me.''

''Somebody else.'' Aleksy spoke over her head to the boy. ''A school friend. Family member, maybe.''

''I could have crashed at my home crib,'' the boy said with a gleam. ''But I didn't want to hang out with associates who are known to the police.''

And score one for the punk.

''You need to call and let your mother know where you are,'' Faye said. ''If she agrees, you can stay here, at least for the night.''

Aleksy didn't have to listen in the kitchen to know the phone call to Jamal's parents did not go well.

When Faye and the boy returned to the living room, she was stiff and unnaturally calm and he was jumpy.

Although the kid's agitation was probably caused more by drugs than by any conversation with his parents, Aleksy thought cynically.

''What's up?'' he asked Faye.

The corners of her pretty mouth tightened. ''He can stay tonight. They'll pick him up at Union Station tomorrow.''

Good, Aleksy wanted to say.

But since his was the minority opinion, he kept his mouth shut. He wasn't a patient man by nature, like his brother Jarek. But his job had taught him that sometimes you had to play the waiting game to win. By tomorrow, the kid would be gone. That was victory enough for now.

Faye summoned a smile for her temporary guest. He was a good-looking kid with a broad, handsome face, but right now he looked sweaty. Twitchy. Uncomfortable.

"Do you want to go wash up?" she asked.

He almost jumped at her offer. "Yeah. Yeah, that would be good."

"Bathroom's down the hall and to the right," she instructed.

"Thanks." He scooped his book bag from the couch and hustled for the door.

Something—his eagerness, maybe, or the way he clutched that bag—tripped Aleksy's internal alarm system.

"Hang on."

The kid froze, face averted, shoulders braced.

Aleksy strolled across the room, ready to grab him if he tried to bolt. "What's in the bag?"

"Nothing." He eased the strap from his shoulder. "Clothes."

"Just clothes?"

"No, man, not just clothes. I got toothpaste and stuff."

In a quick move, Aleksy grasped the bag's dangling strap. "Mind if I have a look?"

His tone was mild, but his grip was steel.

"Why?" Faye asked.

The kid already knew. It was all there in his eyes— the knowledge and the fear, the calculation and the desperate hope. But short of wrestling Aleksy for the bag, there was nothing he could do.

With a resigned shrug, he dropped the bag to the floor. "Be my guest."

It didn't take Aleksy long to find what he was looking for.

He held up the blank prescription bottle half filled with red-and-yellow capsules. "What's this? Cold medicine?"

Faye made a soft, distressed sound.

The kid flinched and dropped his gaze. Maybe he still cared what somebody thought of him.

"What if I said no? What if I said I never saw those before?"

What if?

If the kid got charged with possession a second time, he'd be looking at a hell of a lot more than probation and a fine. Not to mention that Faye would probably never forgive the cop who busted him.

Aleksy stood and pocketed the drugs. "Then I'd have to ask if that book bag was in your possession all day."

It was an out, and the kid, strung out and shaking, was still smart enough to take it.

"I maybe could have left it on the bench at the station. Like, when I went to buy my ticket?"

"I don't have any way of proving you didn't," Aleksy said. "And since I'm not on duty and this isn't my jurisdiction, I'm inclined to believe you."

He walked past the boy to the open bathroom door. Lifting the seat, he emptied the bottle of pills into the toilet and flushed.

"You handled that very well," Faye said as she scraped off their dinner plates into the garbage.

Aleksy fought the surge of satisfaction her approval

gave him. "Yeah, unless he has another stash we don't know about."

Her expression clouded. "Do you really think—"

"No," he said, already regretting his flip remark. Just because he was uncomfortable playing Officer Sensitivity was no reason to worry her. "I don't. But if I catch the kid so much as looking through your medicine cabinet for vitamins, I'm going to bust his butt."

She smiled but gave a significant nod toward the door. "Keep your voice down."

Aleksy stretched plastic wrap over a small bowl of leftover chili. "The kid's crashed in front of the TV. He's not listening to us."

"He must be exhausted." Faye turned from the sink. "You don't need to save that."

Aleksy tightened the plastic. "It's good chili."

Not to mention that he appreciated that with her new painting and two able-bodied men in the house—well, one able-bodied man and a teenage junkie—she had taken the time to prepare and serve the meal. Despite her Goldilocks looks and artsy job, Faye was capable and kind.

Mary Denko had approved, Aleksy remembered. *She's a nice girl,* his mother had whispered as she hugged him good-bye in the hall of Jarek's new house.

The thought filled him with vague panic. He didn't do nice girls.

He thought of Faye, hot and half-naked, straining under him on the dock whispering *Kiss me or die, Detective,* and almost fumbled the bowl.

He'd certainly "done" this one.

"There's not enough there for a meal," Faye said.

"Breakfast?" he suggested.

She laughed and he felt better.

As soon as this case was over, he was going back to his old life in Chicago. Back to chili for breakfast and Chinese for dinner and beer at the end of his shift.

Funny, how quickly his satisfaction faded.

"Anyway, I'm glad Jamal had a good appetite," Faye said as she plunged plates into the soapy water.

Aleksy closed the refrigerator door. "It takes them that way sometimes."

"What?"

"The crash." He hated to disillusion her, but it was better she be prepared. "He'll feel tired. His sleep will be disturbed and he'll either sleep a lot or not at all. Physical movements may speed up or slow down. Amphetamines are pretty unpredictable. He'll be irritable, depressed, anxious…and that will probably start him using again."

"How do you know?"

"I did a couple years on vice."

She shook her head. "I appreciate you have experience with drug users. But how can you predict what Jamal will do? You don't know him."

"Sweetheart, the kid is a junkie."

She whirled on him with wet hands and fiery eyes. "You're doing it again!"

He stared at her, baffled and aggrieved. Why was she so mad? He was trying to help. "Doing what?"

"Reducing him to a label. Do you realize you have not once, since he got here, referred to Jamal by name? It's always 'the kid.' 'The junkie.'" Her chin lifted. "Just the way you typed me as 'the cream puff.'"

Code Zero. Officer safety at risk, use caution.

"I don't do that anymore."

At least, he was pretty sure he didn't. Not to her face. "Right. Now it's 'sweetheart.'" She poked him in the center of his chest with one soapy finger. "That's what you said last night. 'Take me inside, *sweetheart.*'"

"Hey." He was stung. And surprisingly hurt. "I didn't hear you complaining."

"Why would I complain? You're very good at what you do."

"Gee, thanks. But I didn't do it by myself."

"No," she acknowledged. "At first I thought you didn't use my name because it saved you the trouble of remembering who was under you. No embarrassing slipups in the dark if you can call us all 'sweetheart.'"

He started to get angry. "Now, just a—"

"But I think it runs deeper than that. I think you label people so you won't have to deal with them. We're all nice, neat little boxes to you. No messy individual bundles."

"What the hell happened to 'You handled that very well'?"

She removed her finger from his chest. "Well, I—"

"Seems to me if I did have the kid—Jamal," he corrected, "in some kind of box, I would have just charged him with possession."

Faye looked shaken.

Aleksy was glad. He was shaken himself.

"You're right," she said. "I'm sorry."

"You damn well should be."

She glared. "Unless you did it to finesse me into bed."

"Maybe I did." The admission made him furious with both of them. Why should he have to separate out his motives for doing her a good turn? Wasn't it enough to help her? Wasn't it enough to want her? "It didn't work, did it?"

She backed against the sink and crossed her arms

under her breasts. "We'll never know. I'm certainly not sneaking past a seventeen-year-old boy sleeping on my couch to have sex in the guest room."

He frowned. Did she mean if circumstances were different, she would have sex with him?

"We could do it in your room," he offered.

"No, we could not. I won't be pushed into a repeat of last night."

"I'm not trying to push you. If I was, we wouldn't be standing here arguing. I'd do this," he said, and crushed her mouth under his.

He didn't give her time, this time, to resist or argue. He took with familiarity and confidence. His tongue thrust. His mouth demanded.

He was sleek and hard and hot, and Faye's brain shut down, simply surrendering to the onslaught of sensation.

When at last he lifted his head, she was trembling with shock. Outrage, she told herself, but her body gave her the lie. Everything inside her yearned and flowed for him.

Aleksy kept his face close to hers. His breath was hot on her lips. His eyes were dangerous. She felt the rise and fall of his broad chest and was comforted, a little, that he could want her the way he had made her crave him.

"That's what I'd do," he said, biting the words out, "if I was trying to push you into bed."

Chapter 11

Aleksy slept with his door open and his gun handy.

He didn't have a hope in hell that after his he-man demonstration Faye would come tiptoeing across the hall.

The only person in the cottage likely to be moving around at night was Jamal. Maybe Aleksy was guilty of typing, but he didn't trust the kid not to rifle through Faye's possessions searching for drugs or cash or items he could easily lift and sell.

So Aleksy slept lightly.

Because of the kid.

Yeah. And just because every time he closed his eyes his brain got rushed by a hundred images of Faye and the things they'd done and the things he hadn't had a chance to do...

Faye under him, soft and slick, her hips arching to take his thrusts...

Faye straddling him, her hands in his hair and his

hands on her small, perfect breasts, stroking him with her rhythm…

Faye, her eyes, her smile, her body…

Well, anyway, that didn't have anything to do with it.

Just like she didn't want to have anything to do with him.

She thought he was a jerk. A macho jerk who couldn't be bothered to remember her name. A cop jerk who preferred profiling types to getting to know people.

We're all nice, neat little boxes to you. No messy individual bundles.

Wouldn't she laugh to know it was precisely her individuality, the way she consistently defied his definitions and shattered his expectations, that drew him to her?

She was slight and sweet, warm and real, with a sharpness and an inner strength that reminded him of a slim steel blade.

She was also incredibly hot.

And so Aleksy slept lightly and woke up grumpy.

Faye slept poorly and woke with a headache.

She stared in the mirror at her puffy eyes and pale face. What a picture.

She was worried about Jamal, of course.

Her mind churned as she scraped open the drawers of the old dresser. Sometime before she drove him to the station she was going to sit her former student down for a serious chat. She hated the idea of packing him off to his parents today—without his pills, thanks to Aleksy—but with no real plans, either.

Thanks to Aleksy… She sighed.

It was his fault that her arms and legs felt heavy, that

her skin was sensitive to the lightest touch. She almost couldn't bear to put on her clothes. The elastic of her panties chafed and her bra rubbed her nipples.

Her sleep had been invaded and her body aroused by dreams.

By Aleksy, fitting himself between her legs, sliding hard and hot against her, deep and thick inside her...

Aleksy, fully naked, taking time to touch her with his hands, with his mouth, as she arched and writhed on a bed that in her dreams stretched across the room...

Aleksy in her kitchen, his movements quick and his eyes dark with frustration as he said, *I didn't hear you complaining...*

Her mouth set. No. She didn't complain.

She hid.

She yanked a T-shirt over her head and pulled a flowered jumper on top of it. Parading naked was not an option this morning. She was not the kind of woman who flaunted herself. Who flaunted her feelings.

Which made her behavior the other night even more outrageous. *Kiss me or die, Detective.*

She flushed. No wonder Aleksy had run. She'd scared him.

She scared herself.

Beneath the shielding cotton her nipples still peaked. Her skin felt hot and tight. Since Aleksy had moved into her house, she was losing control. Of her life. Of her body. Of her dreams.

Soberly Faye stared at her reflection. With her flyaway blond hair above a tent of flowered fabric, she looked like a little girl playing dress-up in her mother's clothes.

She reached for a hairbrush. She wasn't a little girl anymore, and she'd never been encouraged to indulge in what her mother referred to as nonsense and make-believe.

But she remembered—oh, she remembered—that once upon a time she had dreamed of finding someone who would look at her the way Jarek Denko looked at Tess, with love and admiration in his eyes. Someone who would ask about her work and share the details of his day. Who would tease her while they did the dishes or hold her when she cried or even, maybe, sometimes rub her feet.

Someone who, in her dreams, looked a lot like Aleksy.

In the mirror, the arm holding her hairbrush slowed. She met the troubled eyes of her reflection.

It wasn't only her dreams she had no control over.

It was her heart.

"Where's the kid?" Aleksy asked, tipping back his chair from the breakfast table.

It was strewn with breakfast remains, toast crumbs and egg-smeared plates and sections of the Sunday paper.

Faye regarded him over the top of the entertainment listings. "If you mean Jamal, he's in the bathroom."

Aleksy's mouth quirked. She narrowed her eyes in suspicion. Was he having her on?

But all he said was, "Still?"

"He's a teenager."

"He's a teenage boy."

Faye frowned doubtfully at the plates. Jamal's was nearly half full. "Maybe he isn't feeling well. He wasn't very hungry."

"What's in your medicine cabinet?"

"My...? Oh, no."

The front legs of Aleksy's chair thumped the floor. "I'll just have a look."

He was already out of his seat and headed for the bathroom. Faye didn't have a hope of intercepting him, but she trailed him down the hall.

The shower was silent. No running water splashed in the sink.

Aleksy rapped on the bathroom door. "Hey, kid. You okay?"

Nothing.

He reached for the doorknob.

Faye stopped him, touching her fingers to his chest. Both of them started at the contact.

"Jamal?" she called. "May I come in?"

A grunt answered her.

She looked at Aleksy. When he nodded, she took a deep breath and tried the knob.

The smell of sickness rushed out at them.

Jamal knelt on the linoleum floor, supporting himself with his elbows on the rim of the toilet bowl. His coffee brown skin had an ashy tone. Sweat glazed his face.

"Hey, Harp," he greeted her weakly. "I don't feel so good."

Compassion lurched in her. She touched his shoulder. Under the thin jersey, he was shivering. "So I see. Are you, um, done in here?"

"Dunno. I mean, my stomach is empty for sure, but—" Another spasm racked him.

Faye kept a hand on his shoulder until he was done and then, rinsing a washcloth in warm water, she handed it to him to wipe his face.

"Come on," she said. "Let's get you to bed."

His shoulders hunched. "What if I…"

"I'll bring you a bucket," she promised.

"But I've got to take the train."

"Not today," she said.

Aleksy watched Faye fuss over the boy like a mama wren with a great big cuckoo in the nest. Damn. The kid was a burden she didn't need and a responsibility Aleksy didn't want.

You mean it might be difficult for two unattached adults to have sex with a sick child staying in the same small house.

That, too, Aleksy admitted.

But he definitely was sick, in the throes of withdrawal, shaking so hard he could barely stand. His knuckles gripped the edge of the sink until they turned white. Despite his own weakness and Faye's urging, Jamal was clearly fighting not to lean on her.

Aleksy felt the first faint stirring of respect. Nudging Faye out of the way, he pried the kid's hand from the sink and supported him with his shoulder.

"Let's go," he commanded.

Jamal instinctively obeyed. He was a well-built kid. Not exactly a lightweight. They shuffled into the hall before he asked, "Where we going?"

"You're not going anywhere," Aleksy said grimly. "Except back to bed."

It was Aleksy's tough luck that the only spare bed in the house was already occupied. By him.

Faye left the guest room door open a crack when she returned to the living room.

"He's sleeping now," she informed Aleksy. "Thank you."

He shrugged, uncomfortable with the way she was looking at him, like he was some kind of damn hero or something. And for what? For giving up his bed.

"It's your house," he said. "Your guest room."

"It's still very nice of you," she insisted. "It was your bed."

He didn't deserve her good opinion. "Maybe I figured if you felt sorry enough for me you'd let me share yours."

Instead of firing up at him, she laughed. "No. But nice try, Detective."

He loved her laugh, the way it made her eyes sparkle and showed off her white teeth in a triangular grin, like a cat's. She didn't laugh often enough. Even as he watched, the grin faded and worry took its place.

"I should call the Kings," she said, not moving from the doorway. "They need to know Jamal's not coming home today."

"Want me to do it for you?"

"No." Her slim shoulders squared. "No, it's my responsibility."

Only because she chose to take it on. But he didn't think arguing with her about it would make what she had to do any easier.

And so he sat and listened from the living room as she placed her call.

Outside the sun poured from the sky like a benediction, baking the grass, burnishing the water. It was Sunday morning. Jarek and Tess would be at church with Allie. Suppose the Kings weren't home? Suppose—

Faye's clear voice raised from the kitchen. "Hello, Mr. King?"

They were home. Shoving his hands into his pockets, Aleksy prowled toward the kitchen.

He could hear Faye murmur and stop. "No, I promise you, he— Yes, I did say that, but—"

The rising tension in her voice caught him as surely

as one of Pop's fishhooks and landed him in the kitchen in thirty seconds flat.

Faye was on her feet, her face red and her eyes wide with distress. In two strides, Aleksy reached her and plucked the phone from her slackened grip.

Holding her off with one hand, he put the receiver to his ear.

"—wonder what Principal Carter would say about you shacking up with a good-looking boy like Jamal," a male voice blustered.

Fury burned and leapt in Aleksy like fire. But his voice was deadly cold. "This is Detective Denko. Is this Mr. King?"

"I—who is this?"

"Denko. Chicago PD. Mr. King, were you aware that it's only because of Miss Harper's intervention yesterday that your stepson wasn't arrested and charged a second time with possession of a Class 1 drug?"

"What are you talking about?"

"For a second conviction? Up to two years in prison and a twenty-five-hundred-dollar fine."

"She lied to me. She told me that boy was sick."

"That boy is suffering from amphetamine withdrawal, Mr. King. He's here under my supervision. You are, of course, welcome to come up and I will release him into your custody."

Faye scowled and shook her head vigorously.

Aleksy turned his back on her. "However, unless you leave Jamal here to get clean, I can almost guarantee you he'll be charged."

King swore viciously. "That's blackmail! You're trying to blackmail me."

Well, yeah, Aleksy thought.

"Just doing my job, sir," he said, and cradled the

receiver while King still bellowed on the other end of the line.

Faye waited for him with her arms crossed and the light of battle—or was that amusement?—in her eyes. "Since when does your job include breaking in on private telephone conversations?"

Battle, he concluded.

He shrugged. "You looked like you could stand some help."

"I didn't ask for your help."

"Lucky you. You got it anyway."

"I don't call it helpful to threaten a seventeen-year-old boy with prison."

"Relax. It's not going to happen. I only said that to shake the stepfather loose."

"You still took a risk. What if his parents decided to come get him?"

"Then he'd be their problem."

She arched her eyebrows. "Instead of mine."

"Ours," he said firmly.

Just like that, it popped out, the scariest pronoun in the English language. Ours. As in, our song. Our dog. Our house. Our kids. He started to sweat.

But Faye shook her head again. "Jamal isn't your responsibility."

Grimly Aleksy said, "He is now."

Jamal flung across the room. He was jerky, agitated and angry. Nothing at all like the soft-spoken, good-humored painting companion Faye had taught for three years. Her heart ached for the frustrated young man in front of her even as she mourned that lost child.

"I've got to get out of here," he said.

They'd been having this argument, or one very like

it, over and over for the past twelve hours. It was night.
Faye's energy sank with the sun. But Jamal... She
sighed. Jamal looked ready to go another eight rounds.

"Jamal." She fought to keep her voice reasonable.
"You can't leave. You're still sick."

"I'm good," he insisted.

"You can walk, you mean. That doesn't mean you're
fit to travel. What if you get nauseous on the train?"

"I've just got to go, okay?"

"Go where? Go to what?"

He was silent.

"Why did you come, Jamal?" she asked quietly.

He dropped on the edge of the mattress—the springs
creaked under his weight—and dropped his head in his
hands. "You don't understand. I thought I could shake
it but I can't." He lifted his anguished face. "Harp, I
need to take something."

She stood, feeling hopelessly inadequate. "I'll get
you some juice. And some aspirin."

"I don't need your—" he used an ugly word "juice
and aspirin. I'm telling you, I need something."

She hesitated. "If you agreed to go into a program—"

"Screw that."

"There are medicines that can help you feel better."

"There are pills that can make me feel better, and I
can score them a damn sight faster than I can check into
some loser program."

Aleksy cut in. "If you feel that way about it, I can
drive you back to Chicago tonight."

Faye turned. He lounged in the doorway, his face
hard, his voice hard, his eyes hard.

The boy looked at him warily. "You mean it?"

"No," said Faye.

"Sure," Aleksy said. "Think about it. Drop you off on any street corner and you can be high in a couple of hours. Of course, you'll be picked up in a couple of days and dead within a couple of years, but if that's what you want… Is that what you want, Jamal?"

Jamal stared at him, stone-faced.

Faye's heart hammered. "I don't think he's in any condition to decide—"

"Butt out, Faye," Aleksy said without looking at her. "He's got to decide or it's no good."

Jamal's shoulders bunched. So did his hands. "Don't you talk to her like that."

Aleksy smiled. Not a nice smile. Faye's insides curled. "I can talk to her any way I want. Unless you think you're man enough to stop me."

Jamal lunged across the room, catching Aleksy around the waist and ramming him into the door frame. Faye yelped. They rolled to the floor, the tall, furious teenager flailing and the lean, tough cop struggling to contain him.

Jamal's sneaker connected hard with her shin. Helpless, angry, she staggered back, tears starting to her eyes. They crashed into the dresser and she bumped into the bed. The lamp toppled to its side, knocking the shade askew.

"Stop it!"

They did.

At least, Aleksy pinned Jamal, and then lurched to his feet, hauling the boy up after him.

Grabbing a fistful of Bears jersey, he thrust his face into Jamal's. "The only reason I'm not going to mop the floor with you is you showed some kind of guts, sticking up for her. Now why don't you do something for her that actually matters." He gave the boy a shake and released him. "I'm going out for some air. Let me know what you decide about that ride."

Jamal stood nursing his jaw until Aleksy stalked down the hall.

"Bastard," he muttered.

Faye's knees wobbled. She sat. "Are you hurt?"

"No." Jamal's tongue poked his cheek as he explored his teeth. "Not really."

That was something.

She took a careful breath. "What are you going to do now?"

The teen looked at her, surprised. "Well, I can't go off now, can I?" he said in a disgusted tone. "That dude is crazy. I can't leave you alone with him."

Aleksy stared across the water at Freer's place. Two boats bobbed at their moorings, barely visible gleams in the dark—a big one with a motor and a little one with a mast. Sleek and ostentatious, but neither one beyond the legitimate means of a reputable gun dealer from northern Illinois. Neither one belonging to a mysterious visitor from Canada. Aleksy knew. He'd run their registration numbers already.

Frustration cramped his stomach and constricted his jaw. He was wasting his time here.

In more ways than one.

"You were a little rough on Jamal back there," Faye observed behind him, her voice mild as the night.

If anything, his jaw got tighter. So did his gut. "I was rough on both of you. Want me to apologize?"

She came to stand beside him at the rail. Her blond hair was almost silver in the dark. Her smell, sweet and light, reached inside him and made him shiver.

"Would you?" she asked curiously.

"Hell, I don't know. Is he staying?"

Her lips curved. "Yes."

"Then, no."

She laughed, which eased his mind and screwed the tension in his body up another notch.

He turned to face her, leaning his hips against the rail. "Of course, I might reconsider. If you begged me."

She tilted her head. "Begged you," she repeated slowly, as if she were tasting the idea.

He grinned, enjoying the game. Enjoying her. "Yeah."

Her gaze lowered to his mouth. She touched her tongue to her bottom lip, and a zing went through his system.

"For…?" she murmured.

His mind had fogged. "What?"

"What should I beg you for?"

"Anything you want," he said hoarsely. "I'm a generous guy. Given the right inducement."

She drew her fingers along his arm. "I'll have to keep that in mind."

Oh, man. He'd had her twisting under him not twenty yards from this spot, not twenty-four hours ago. Could he get that lucky again?

And then she turned to the water and sighed. "He's not doing so well, is he?"

Not tonight. His mind processed that, accepted it, even as his body struggled with disappointment.

"Jamal? The first couple of days are the worst. He gets through them, he could be okay. How long has he been using?"

"Five months." It was the first time she had admitted the problem, faced the problem, without evasion or excuse. Was she even aware of it? Aleksy was. "He started using those caffeine pills to study for finals. I don't know when the pills stopped working and he started buying drugs on the street.''

"Chances are he didn't get hooked right away. Which would explain why his symptoms are fairly mild.''

She nodded. ''It's just that nothing I can do seems to help.''

"Honey, nothing anybody can do would help right now. His normal reward system isn't working.'' He dug back into his narcotics training for an explanation that would satisfy her. ''Amphetamines bypass the normal triggers—like food and friendship and sleep and sex—and go straight for the brain's pleasure center. To compensate, the brain's natural chemistry shuts down.''

Her brow furrowed. ''Which means what, exactly?''

"Which means your basic junkie needs the drug even more to feel good.'' Aleksy shrugged. ''It'll take a while for Jamal's brain to recover and for normal rewards to work again, that's all.''

She stood on tiptoe and brushed soft lips across his cheek.

"Hey.'' His heart jerked. He was absurdly pleased. "What was that for?''

"That was to thank you.'' There was a smile in her voice as she added, ''Consider it a normal reward.''

She turned until she was standing directly in front of him, the yellow light from the house making a halo of her hair. She put her arms around his neck and the night slowed around them while his pulse went into overdrive. The hem of her skirt brushed his jeans. The tips of her breasts touched his chest.

He swallowed hard. If he were the nice guy she thought he was, he would step back.

He didn't move.

She did.

She kissed him again, slowly, balancing herself with her hands on his shoulders. Her eyes were open. His eyes were, too. He saw her delicate features blur as she leaned forward and the silvery gleam of starlight on her cheeks and brow. He felt her lips and the tip of her tongue, and the weight of her, light and warm in his arms, and the taste of her, sweet and hot on his mouth, bypassed his usual defenses and went directly to his pleasure center.

He couldn't stand it.

He crushed her against him and took and *took,* everything she had to offer, all her sweetness, all her light, all her warmth. He plunged his tongue into her mouth, he pressed her hips to his, and instead of telling him to get lost, to get a grip, she skimmed her hands up and down his back as if she couldn't get enough of him.

It was enough to make a guy a little crazy, especially if he knew that under her tentlike dress and soft cotton shirt, she was slight and silky and perfect.

Only…

A new thought intruded on his moonstruck brain.

Only he'd already taken her once on the dock without even bothering to slip her out of her clothes. Without taking the time to see her naked or tell her she was beautiful or worship her breasts with his mouth.

Yeah, before he made love to Faye again, he wanted time. And a bed. He definitely wanted a bed next time.

He dragged the strength from somewhere to bracelet her wrists with his hands and pull her arms from around his neck. He pressed a kiss into the center of each palm. Her fingers stroked his face and the reminder of all he was passing up nearly made him change his mind.

"I, uh—" Jeez, he didn't know what to say. He'd sure as hell never said "no" before. "You should maybe go in. Check on the kid."

She studied him a moment, her big eyes questioning in the moonlight. "That's a very good excuse," she said. "Who is it for?"

"Just be a good girl," he begged, "and run along."

She angled her head. "Maybe I'm tired of running. I can almost guarantee you I'm tired of being good."

All the blood left his brain and rushed directly to his groin, which made it really tough to think.

Did she mean it?

Did he want her to?

The uncertainty was killing him.

There were worse ways to die.

Chapter 12

"I'm not going to touch that thing."

Aleksy tried to hide his frustration. "It's not going to bite you."

"It's wiggling!"

"Of course it's wiggling. Otherwise it wouldn't attract anything."

Jamal watched Aleksy bait his hook with the worm and throw both into the water. "Man, that's obscene. I think I'm going to throw up."

"You've *been* throwing up," Aleksy said testily. "An hour or two fishing isn't going to make it any worse."

Jamal squirmed around, trying to get comfortable against his tree.

Aleksy had picked a spot where the bank fell sharply and the water flowed cool and deep. Despite the late hour—it was almost ten, and the sun was well over the trees—he figured they had a shot at a catfish, maybe some bluegills.

"So some guys actually do this, like, for fun, huh?"

Aleksy stretched his neck to get the kinks out. "That's the idea."

"Well, it's a stupid idea," Jamal said.

Aleksy was beginning to agree with him.

But this morning, observing Faye's pale face and tired eyes, her strained smile and weary patience, he thought she could use a break. The kid might be the artistic genius she claimed. But with his system still jangling from the effects of withdrawal, he was also a real pain in the ass.

Aleksy baited the kid's hook and handed back his rod. "See if you can drop your line by that log over there."

"Why?"

"You might catch a catfish."

The boy looked briefly interested. "Like, to eat?"

"Yeah. We could fry it for dinner. Channel cats are good eating."

"I'll probably puke it up."

"Probably. But I won't."

Jamal turned his face away, but not before Aleksy saw the grin that transformed him from sullen punk into nice kid. He flicked his pole over the water and caught his hook on the log.

He swore.

"Reel it in," Aleksy said. "Try again. Not so hard this time. Right by the—that's it."

Jamal jiggled the pole. "What do I do now?"

"Wait."

"How long?"

"Until you feel something on the line."

"That worm drowns, it won't be so attractive any-more," the boy said darkly.

This time it was Aleksy who turned away to hide his grin. "Don't worry about it. Catfish aren't choosy."

"How come you know all this stuff?"

"My pop used to take me fishing. When I was a kid. Now shut up or you'll scare the fish away."

That silenced the teen for all of about two minutes. He wasn't shaking as badly today, but he obviously had trouble keeping still. He shifted again against his tree.

"You got any kids?" he asked.

Aleksy sighed. "No." And at the moment he knew why.

"Me, either."

Aleksy didn't bother pointing out that, at seventeen, Jamal was far too young to be a father. In his neigh-borhood, younger kids were made fathers every day.

"So, you married?" Jamal persisted.

"Why? You want to ask me out?"

"Funny, man." But Jamal didn't sound amused. His voice still wasn't steady but his eyes were. Steady, and surprisingly adult. "What are you doing with Harp?"

Aleksy's line bobbed. It was a good question. He didn't have any idea how to answer it.

"Why?" he asked again. "You want to ask *her* out?"

Red crept up the boy's cheekbones. His mouth set.

Oh, hell, Aleksy thought, alarmed by the mess he'd stumbled into.

He should have seen it coming. Faye was young and pretty. She was sharp and funny and warm and kind. She had encouraged Jamal to pursue interests and dreams few people probably even understood.

More than all that, she cared. Of course the kid had a major jones for her.

Talk about your can of worms…

"It's not like that," Jamal said with painful dignity. "Harp is, like, a *friend.* She knows a lot about art and stuff, but about some things she's kind of clueless. So as her friend, I'm asking—are you two doing it?"

Damn. Eric Denko couldn't have done a better job of demanding his intentions. Aleksy didn't know whether to swear or give the kid a gold star.

He should say yes, to protect his cover.

He should say no, to protect Faye.

What he said was, "I don't think that's any of your business."

Jamal snorted. "Man, that is so lame."

Yeah. It was.

Faye heard them argue as they approached the house.

"I'm not cleaning any fish," Jamal said. "I don't know how."

"You'll have to learn, then, won't you?" Aleksy asked. He sounded amused.

Jamal expressed his opinion of that in one short, ripe phrase and Faye smiled. They sounded so…normal, she decided. Surely that was good?

Footsteps climbed the plank steps and crossed the wooden deck. The screen scraped open.

She looked up from her seat on the floor and saw Aleksy, big and dark against the hot, bright day outside. He smelled of sun and water and, faintly, of fish. His hair was ruffled by the wind. His shirt clung to him in the heat.

The light behind him dazzled her. He dazzled her.

She felt summer unfolding warm and low inside her, and caught her breath.

His quick gaze swept the mess around her and settled on her face. "How's it going?"

She smiled ruefully. "Well—"

"Whoa, Harp." Jamal checked himself before he planted his foot on a half-finished cloud study. "Looks like a starving artists' sale in here."

"Productive morning?" Aleksy asked.

"Not really," she confessed. "I thought I'd use the time while you were gone to work. Only when I started to pull things out to work on, there wasn't really... I couldn't decide... How was yours?"

He shrugged. "Not bad. Two bluegills. Kid here's going to clean them."

"Yeah, right," Jamal muttered.

Aleksy stepped carefully over a pile of discarded sketches. "Fishermen's rules, kid. You catch 'em, you clean 'em."

Faye widened her eyes in admiration. "Jamal! You caught them?"

His shoulders straightened. "Yeah. Both of them," he added, with a smug glance at Aleksy. "So, I'm thinking, since I did all the work so far, the cop should do something."

"Nice try," said Aleksy. "Only it doesn't work that way. You need to learn to finish what you start."

"That sounds reasonable to me," Faye said.

"Oh, yeah?" Jamal sauntered through the paintings scattered on the floor. "So what did you get done this morning?"

She flushed. "Besides the breakfast dishes? Nothing."

Instead, she sat, with the whole bright, empty morning stretching before her and a dozen promising beginnings spread out around her, and let herself be paralyzed by the possibilities. Frozen by the fear of the wrong choice, she'd made no choice at all. Only excuses.

There was a sorry parallel there to the rest of her life lately that she didn't want to examine too closely.

"I didn't know what I should work on."

"If somebody in class said that, you'd be all over them," Jamal observed, dropping onto the couch. "You always told us you can't make the shot you never take."

Aleksy lifted one eyebrow. "Sports analogies? I'm impressed."

"Don't be." Her reply was too sharp and too revealing. She tried to soften it with a smile. "I didn't even get in the game this morning."

"There's still time," Aleksy said.

"Excuse me?"

"You've got all afternoon. The kid and I are cooking dinner. Why don't you go ahead and paint something?"

"Paint something."

"Yeah."

"Just like that."

"Yeah. Why not?"

Because I'm an artist, you clod, she wanted to tell him. *I need to be in the mood to create something.*

Only wasn't that precisely the attitude she was always fighting in her students?

She looked around at her abandoned landscapes. That old ranger station reaching above the tree line had some promise, or those clouds scudding above the choppy water...

"I suppose I could work for a little while," she said without enthusiasm.

"You do that. Jamal, get the newspaper. We've got fish to clean."

"Oh, man." But the teenager shambled toward the kitchen.

Faye stood, every bit as mutinous and even more unsure, wavering between Aleksy's expectations and her own doubts.

He cocked his head, slid her a grin. "Problem, cream puff?"

Her breath hissed. Even when she saw quite clearly what he was doing, she was incapable of resisting his challenge.

"No," she said. "Nothing I can't handle."

The fish turned out perfect, white and moist in a crisp golden crust. Jamal had two helpings and didn't even throw up.

Faye slid one last morsel onto her own plate. "Did you ever get a fishing license?" she asked Aleksy.

He nodded. "Cost me fourteen bucks."

"Fourteen?" Jamal said. "Man, for that kind of dough we could have gotten steaks."

"Yes, but then you would have missed out on the whole he-man-hunter experience," Faye said.

The teenager shrugged. "I could've shot the cow."

Aleksy grinned. "Yeah, but would you clean it?"

Faye enjoyed their banter. But sometime between clearing the table and sitting on the deck with her coffee, she began to notice gaps in the conversation, looming holes that they ignored, things they did not say.

Jamal ducked any discussion of the future. It wasn't simply that he didn't want to talk about his plans for the coming academic year. He didn't want to talk about what he was doing tomorrow. He excused himself early—"That he-man-hunter thing takes it out of a guy"—and went to bed.

"He's still crashing," Aleksy said in response to Faye's worried look. "This morning he couldn't get it together to tie his own fishing line. He definitely can't talk to you now."

"I am very easy to talk to," she protested.

He lifted an eyebrow slightly. His resemblance to his brother Jarek in that moment was startling.

"Aren't I?"

"Yeah. You are. Leave it alone, Faye," he said, and went outside.

She flinched. Now that she had stopped hiding, Aleksy was finding reasons to avoid her.

She wanted more than I could give. To her or any woman.

Faye didn't know what to do about that yet. She didn't know what she could do. She wasn't even sure what she wanted to do.

But she wasn't going to take his dismissal lying down. In the morning, she and Jamal were going to have a few things out.

"You could layer some gray in on those clouds," Jamal offered over her shoulder.

So he was awake, she thought hopefully. That was good.

He was paying attention. Even better.

Faye dipped her brush in the water, carefully nonchalant. "I don't know. I don't want to build up too much paint."

He shrugged. "Then you lift it out with a sponge. No biggie. Give it a chance."

She had taught him that, she thought with mild pride. It remained to be seen what else she could teach him.

"So you figure if you make a mistake, you can correct it?" she asked.

He met her gaze, instantly wary. "Uh-uh," he said. "I don't want to talk about it."

"If you really didn't want to talk about it, you wouldn't have come to find me."

He was silent.

Faye sighed. Tried again. "All right. What do you want?"

"I want everybody to leave me alone."

"Not happening," Faye said. "Jamal, you have to face this. You can't run away from your problems."

"Why not?" His voice was bitter. Resentful. "You did."

His attack left her momentarily speechless. She drew a careful breath. "Is that how it felt to you?"

He stared at her with a man's closed, accusing face and a child's hurt and hopeful eyes.

"All right," she said. "Okay. Maybe it felt that way to me, too. But I didn't just drop you on this one, Jamal. There's a difference between quitting and being defeated."

"What difference?" he said. "Either way, you left."

Faye ached inside. "Well… If you're defeated—like an army, you know?—you can sometimes retreat and, and regroup and go back to the fight."

"Is that what you're going to do?"

She thought about it. Unbidden, Aleksy's comment came back to her. *I bet you were a hell of a teacher.*

"Yes," she decided. A huge weight lifted from her chest. The relief of it made her almost dizzy. "Yes, I am. What about you?"

He shook his head. "They won't let me take that scholarship, Harp. I'm the first kid ever in my family to have a shot at college. Mama doesn't want me to throw that away. And Ron says if I'm not going to get a job, I've got to study something practical."

"Then we'll sit down with your mother and Ron and the guidance counselor and find a middle way. There have got to be schools that offer both business and art."

"That doesn't help me this year. I've still got to choose electives. And if I take all the college prep courses, there's no time for art."

The fact that he was even considering his options was encouraging.

"I'll make you a deal," Faye said. "You agree to some kind of treatment program, and I'll give you lessons after school, anytime, for free."

He looked away. "I'll think about it," he said.

She tried to take hope from that.

And the gray wash worked. The clouds breathed and brooded over a fluid landscape.

Faye took a step back to study her painting. She actually liked the movement of the sky and the pattern of the water. And that boat in the corner, with its sails half unfurled, ready to lift to the wind and go—

Aleksy spoke suddenly behind her and her heart gave a wild, undisciplined leap. "Jarek said there are a bunch of boats coming into the marina. For some kind of race this weekend. Want to go down, grab an ice cream, take a look?"

She turned to glare, which was hard to pull off while her pulse was pounding in a so-glad-to-see-you rhythm. What was with him? What did he want? After avoiding her all morning, he expected her to drop everything and go with him into town?

"Why?" she asked baldly. "Do you need cover to go look at the boats?"

His brows drew together. "I might have an interest in the boats." He nodded toward her painting. "I thought you might, too."

She was stunned. Disarmed. Confused.

She ran her fingers through her hair. "I don't need to look at a lot of boats to paint this one. I have photographs."

He caught her hand and linked his fingers with hers. "Then come for the ice cream."

He smiled at her and her insides melted and her day went all yellow, like that scene in *South Pacific* shot through a colored lens.

Aleksy raised his voice. "Hey, Jamal!"

"He's sleeping," Faye said, still thawing but fighting it.

"What?" the boy yelled back groggily from his bedroom

"We're going into town."

"Have fun."

"You're coming with us."

Faye tried to find a thought in the puddle her mind had become. "Is that a good idea? He needs his sleep."

Aleksy slanted a look down at her. "Better if he sleeps at night."

Her breath caught. "Better for who?"

Jamal shuffled into the room, scowling. "Why do I have to come? You trying to keep tabs on me?"

"No," Aleksy said. "I really want a chaperone along on our date."

"It's not a date," Faye said.

They didn't date, she thought with a twist of heart. They had sex on the dock.

But later, ambling down Harbor Street under the flags and the awnings, with the tourists browsing the windows and the local skateboarders jumping the curbs, she had to admit it felt like a date. The kind of date other people seemed to have, the kind that belonged between the covers of a romance novel.

Aleksy waited for her while she stopped in the drugstore and the camera shop. He bought her a blueberry ice cream from the Rose Farms Café. He held her hand.

It was wonderful. Surreal.

"I feel like a white guy in a P. Diddy video," Jamal grumbled behind them. "I thought the lady in the ice-cream store was going to ask me for ID."

"If you wanted to mess with her mind, you could have ordered vanilla," Aleksy said.

Faye counted one heartbeat, two, and then Jamal laughed.

"Rocky Road, man," he said. "I'm all about nuts and chocolate."

Faye let herself hope. He was eating again. He was laughing again. Maybe, in time, he would make a recovery. Maybe, in time, she could...

Oops. The sun burned the top of her head and melted the ice cream in her hand. She stopped on the sidewalk to chase the drip with her tongue.

"Well, isn't that a pretty sight."

Richard Freer smiled from the entrance to his shop. A huge American flag hung in the window behind the "Liberty" sign. Both the glass and his shoes were polished.

Faye never knew what to do with comments like that,

the ones that left you violated and wondering. Was he being deliberately offensive? Or was she overreacting?

She forced herself to smile back. "Hi, Richard."

"Enjoying your ice cream?"

Aleksy inserted his shoulder between them. "We were just on our way down to the marina."

"I didn't know you were a boat person."

"She isn't," Aleksy answered shortly.

Faye appreciated his support but she didn't want any awkwardness spoiling their afternoon. "I had a few errands to run," she said lightly.

"Good for you. Support the local businesses, I always say." Richard switched his attention to Aleksy. "You haven't been in to see those handguns."

"No. Not yet."

"You ought to take a look. I've got a couple of .38s that would probably suit you."

"Another time."

"Sure. Anytime." Richard looked Faye up and down. "I can see you're busy."

Aleksy took her arm. "Well, it's been swell, but we've got to go now."

He steered Faye down the sidewalk. Classic territorial male behavior, she thought, and wasn't sure if she were miffed or flattered.

"Wherever we're going better have some place to sit down," Jamal said.

Aleksy turned to look at him. "Where were you a minute ago?"

Jamal shrugged. "Around. Old white guys with guns make me nervous."

"Yeah," Aleksy said grimly. "Me, too."

Faye tripped as realization struck. "Is he the one?"

Aleksy tightened his grip on her elbow. "Watch your step."

She shook free. She should have seen it before, she thought. If she hadn't been so eager to avoid involvement, so worried about Jamal, so blindsided by lust, she would have seen it before. But Richard Freer…he knew her aunt, for heaven's sake.

She craned her neck to look back at him. "What did he do?"

Aleksy propelled her to the end of the street. "Not here," he said.

That made sense. Reluctantly she gave up looking over her shoulder.

The road dead-ended at Front Street. A strip of park no more than a few yards wide separated the street from the boardwalk. Beyond the faded grass and a granite slab inscribed with the names of the town's war dead, boats bobbed at their moorings. Gulls wheeled and cried over the open water. Faye lifted her face to the breeze.

"Hey, there's a bench," said Jamal.

Faye looked him over with a teacher's experienced eye. He was doing much better today. Still, his face gleamed with sweat. And he'd gone fishing this morning. Maybe it would be better if he—

"Why don't you sit down?" she said.

"Yeah. Maybe I'll do that."

She watched him cross to the bench and then turned on Aleksy. "Now you can tell me what's going on."

"Did you know you have ice cream on your hand?"

She blinked. "What?"

He removed the drugstore bag and the camera shop bag from her grasp and tucked them under his arm. Catching the hand that held her ice-cream cone, he brought it to his lips. "Here," he said. His warm mouth sucked gently at the base of her thumb. "And here."

His tongue dabbed between her fingers. Her system jolted. Her breathing hitched.

"Don't try to distract me," she said.

His dark eyes watched her over their clasped hands. "Is it working?"

Too well.

"Not at all," she said crossly.

He released her hand. "Can't blame a guy for trying."

"Aleksy—"

"You're better off not knowing."

"Look, pal." The finger that he'd licked stabbed the center of his chest. "I'm a teacher. This 'ignorance is bliss' routine doesn't cut it with me."

"What about 'I don't want to be involved'?"

She sucked in her breath. No more running, she thought. No more evasion. "Maybe I've changed my mind about that."

"And maybe I haven't."

"Well." She exhaled shakily. "That's clear, at least."

He'd hurt her, Aleksy saw with instant regret. He'd always accepted that he would.

What he hadn't guessed was that her pain would tear him, too.

"Faye."

She turned and walked away from him, down the boardwalk. The wind pushed at her long flowered skirt and feathered her hair. Panic hit him. She was leaving. Women never left him. Not without long, deliberate effort on his part, anyway.

"Damn it, Faye!"

She didn't look back.

Jamal loped up beside him. "Man, what did you say to Harp? She looks pissed."

"I didn't say anything," Aleksy growled.

Which may have been the problem. This whole communication thing sucked.

He set his jaw and went after her.

Chapter 13

He found her in the Blue Moon, perched on a bar stool, nursing a beer and flirting with Mark DeLucca.

Damn quick recovery.

DeLucca was wiping the bar with long, slow strokes, and Faye was staring at him like he was a painting in a museum. The guy even looked like a painting, his face barely rescued from pretty boy perfection by his black eyebrows and slightly crooked nose.

Somebody, sometime, had broken it for him.

Aleksy would have liked to take a poke at it himself.

DeLucca saw him by the door and murmured something to Faye that made her swivel around on her bar stool.

She looked at him and her chin went up.

Aleksy scowled. Fine. If she wanted to play this mad, he had plenty of experience as the heavy.

Although he'd never actually assumed the role opposite a woman he still wanted.

He stalked to the bar and slid onto the stool next to hers. "Give me a Miller on draft," he ordered DeLucca.

The bartender raised his eyebrows. "Aren't you going to ask if that seat is taken?"

"Butt out," Aleksy snarled.

"Only if the lady tells me to."

"It's all right," Faye said. "I can handle—"

So help him, if she said "him," he was going to break something.

"—things," she said. She turned to Aleksy. "What do you want?"

Damned if he knew.

He took a swig of his beer. "You left kind of suddenly back there."

Her big brown eyes were cool. Her voice was frosty. "Were you worried I was leaving you with responsibility for Jamal?"

He tried to chip his way through the ice. "Jamal can take care of himself. I was worried about you."

"You don't need to. I'm a big girl, Detective." She hitched her canvas bag on her shoulder and dropped a five on the bar. "I'll go keep Jamal company while you finish your beer."

"I'll go with you."

"No, you stay." She might as well have said it to a dog. She slipped from her stool. "Thanks, Mark. I'll see both of you later."

He watched her march to the door, slim and indomitable in her flowered skirt and flat sandals.

DeLucca shook his head. "You are in such deep—"

"Tell me about it," Aleksy said.

The bartender took a final swipe with his rag. "So, who's this Jamal? Old boyfriend?"

"Nope. One of her kids."

Mark sent another look after the slight figure in the flowered skirt. "She must be older than she looks."

"She's a teacher."

"Elementary?"

"No." With an unaccustomed feeling of pride, Aleksy said, "She teaches art at a high school on the south side."

"Well, that explains it," Mark said.

"Explains what?"

"What she's doing with you. Obviously the lady likes hard cases."

"Very funny." Aleksy took another pull of his beer.

"So, the kid followed her up here?"

"Yeah." Aleksy watched, brooding, as Mark filled a bowl with peanuts. "He screws up big time and then shows up hoping she'll take him in. Which of course she does, seeing as she is just about the warmest, sweetest woman in the world and a total sucker."

"Lucky for him," Mark observed.

Aleksy frowned. "Yeah."

Mark moved to the other end of the bar to take an order from a couple of guys in polo shirts and over-priced shoes. When he came back he said, "Lucky for you, too."

Aleksy narrowed his eyes. "You got something to say to me, DeLucca?"

The bartender shrugged and filled two mugs with draft. "Just that sooner or later most of us need somebody who will give us a second chance. The kid. Me. You."

"You learn that in bartending school?"

"No," Mark said. He didn't offer to elaborate.

And Aleksy didn't ask. He had troubles enough of his own.

On the other hand, DeLucca kind of had a point there. So when he got back from serving the polo shirts, Aleksy said, "You've got a lot of tourists in. For mid-week, I mean."

It was an olive branch, cautiously extended.

Warily, Mark accepted it. "Our share. They come up early for the owners' day regatta at the Algonquin."

"You race?"

Mark's eyes gleamed. "Not that one."

"Why not?" Aleksy asked, genuinely curious now.

"That one's for the Sunday sailors."

Aleksy put it all together—the quiet scorn, the tattoo… "Navy?" he guessed.

Mark smiled thinly. "Marines."

Well, hell. "Afghanistan?"

"Toward the end of my tour, yeah."

The bar door banged open. Jamal stood in the entryway, taking great gulps of air.

"Denko! Man, come quick! Some bastard knocked Harp down and snatched her purse."

"And you're sure you didn't see his face at all?" Jarek Denko asked gently.

Faye struggled to concentrate. Her palms stung. Her wrist throbbed.

Mark DeLucca had cleaned her hands and bandaged her wrist with surprising skill and compassion. He was trained as a first responder, he'd told her, when Aleksy first brought her into the bar.

But despite the tape's support and the bag of ice he'd plopped on her wrist, the pain of the old fracture was bad enough to be distracting.

"Damn it, Jare, we've been over this," Aleksy snapped. He prowled forward, hands thrust in his pockets, violence simmering in his eyes. "The son of a bitch pushed her from behind. All she saw was the ground. And his back when he took off."

"And there was nothing about his back that caught your attention?" Jarek continued, undisturbed by his brother's outburst. "Nothing unusual about his clothes, for instance?"

Faye closed her eyes, trying to filter details of the snatching through the pulse of pain and the shock of reaction. "Dark pants, navy shirt and a—gray?—ball cap. Nothing unusual. He wore sneakers," she offered, opening her eyes. "He was very ordinary, really. Medium height, medium build, medium complexion. His hair was dark, I think."

"But there was nothing familiar about him?" Jarek persisted.

"No. I'm sorry," she said, feeling inadequate. "I don't know many people in town."

Jarek's smile warmed his cool gray eyes. "Very understandable."

"Woman from the hardware store was a witness," Aleksy said. His voice still had an edge. "Marcia somebody. I wrote it down."

"Tompkins?"

"That's the one."

"Well, that's good. If your thief was a local, Marcia will know him." Jarek sighed and stood. "But I'm sorry to say it's just as likely you were robbed by someone passing through."

"Lots of visitors right now, with the regatta coming up," Mark volunteered from over by the bar.

"Are you done with her?" Aleksy asked abruptly. "Can I take her home now?"

Jarek nodded. "Unless you'd like to stop by the hospital."

Faye blinked. "What? Oh, no." She flexed her wrist experimentally. It hurt, but she was used to that. And she wanted to go home, back to the cottage that had been her escape and her refuge. She wanted to crawl in her hole and pull it in after her, like in the cartoons.

"About your purse." Jarek cleared his throat. "There's a good chance we'll get it back for you. The thief probably dumped it somewhere. After he took your cash and credit cards."

"My credit cards." She sat upright on the bar's hard wooden chair. "I have to—"

"We will." Aleksy's hand, hard and reassuring, closed on her shoulder. "After we get you home."

He was as good as his word. He loaded Faye, Jamal and the ice bag into his TransAm. He gave them a choice between Chinese and fast food and then picked up dinner at the drive through window of the local Burger Barn. While Faye made phone calls canceling her credit cards, Aleksy nudged Jamal into the shower and off to bed. Shaky from a combination of excitement and drug withdrawal, Jamal crashed with only a token protest.

Faye frowned thoughtfully as Aleksy gathered the teenager's clothes and dumped them into her aunt's old washing machine.

He was supportive.

He was practical.

He was efficient.

And he did everything with a tight-lipped temper that made her long to wring his neck. She hadn't purposefully thrown herself in harm's way to force him to take care of her.

When he banged shut the lid of the washing machine, she hung up the phone.

"Come talk to me," she suggested.

Tight with tension, he stood before her, his thumbs hooked in the belt loops of his jeans. He looked gorgeous. Dangerous. Hot.

"What do you need?" he asked.

Like a match to paper, his heat licked along the edge of her nerves. "I don't need anything. I wanted to apologize."

"What for?"

"Well…" She waved her hands. Clumsily, because of her bandaged wrist. "You didn't exactly move in expecting to be saddled with laundry and patient care."

"No. I moved in figuring I could stake out my suspect and maybe get laid at the same time. Tell me again what the hell you have to apologize for."

She frowned. This conversation wasn't going the way she planned at all. She was supposed to be calming him. Instead he was…well, he was ticking her off.

"Okay, maybe apologize was the wrong word. I should have said I wanted to thank you."

"What for?" he repeated.

Was she supposed to present him with an itemized list?

"Everything."

"Jarek is going after the guy who robbed you. DeLucca bandaged your wrist. What are you thanking me for, Faye?"

She was genuinely baffled. And hurt. "Why are you being like this?"

"Maybe I don't like being useless."

Warmth bloomed in her chest. She should have

guessed Aleksy would try to take responsibility for her—for her safety, for her comfort—on himself.

"You're not useless," she said. As if that would convince him. She took a deep breath and continued painfully. "After I—after it, you know, happened, I was on the ground. And I was, well, so surprised, and my wrist hurt, and I wasn't thinking very clearly."

Faye gave a little shiver. It wasn't very pleasant, even now, to remember. "But I do remember thinking that it would be all right, that you would come. And then I looked up—" she did so now, smiling "—and there you were."

His gaze darkened. "You don't expect enough from me," he said roughly.

She kept her voice light. She told herself she knew what he wanted. And what he didn't want.

"This has to be the first time you've said *that* to a woman," she teased.

He didn't smile back. In his eyes, she read his frustration and an echo of her own confusion. And something else, something that quickened her heartbeat against her ribs.

His fingertips skimmed her cheek. "I should take better care of you," he muttered.

She was touched more deeply than she wanted to admit. "Well," she said slowly, "you could take care of my knees."

"What are you talking about?"

"My knees. When I fell this afternoon, I landed on my hands and knees." She lifted her skirt to show him.

He swore. "Why didn't you say anything?"

"I didn't really notice at the time. They didn't hurt. Not like my hands or my wrist."

He scowled. "They're bleeding."

"Not anymore."

"They could still get infected."

His scolding made her smile. His concern fissured her heart. "That's why I need you to take care of them. In fact, now that I think about it, it's the least you can do. I took care of yours."

"Come on," he said abruptly. "You need to clean these up."

But when she followed him into the bathroom, he wouldn't let her do a thing. He made her sit on the toilet and knelt between her legs. Rinsing a washcloth in the sink, he gently sponged the dirt from her scrapes.

The soap seeped in and stung. She must have made some sound, because he lifted the washcloth.

"All right?"

"I'm fine," she assured him, loving the concern in his voice. "I'm tough."

"You're a cream puff," he said.

But his fingers, as he smoothed the antibiotic ointment on her knees, trembled.

He looked up and caught her watching him and flushed darkly. "I don't like seeing you get hurt."

He looked so sweet, angry and embarrassed. She could smell the scent of her shampoo on his hair and feel the heat of his body, close between her thighs. She wanted him to kiss her. Why didn't he kiss her?

"I'm fine," she said again. "Anyway, we match now."

"How's that?" he asked, but he sounded distracted.

"Our knees," she said, leaning forward so that her breasts approached his mouth. His breath was hot. Her nipples tightened. She wondered if he could tell. "We'll have matching scars."

Aleksy swallowed hard. He could see everything—

everything—through that damn T-shirt. Didn't she know? Or didn't she care?

She didn't need this.

She didn't want him.

She wanted the man she'd made him out to be, the caring, sharing protector type. The kind of guy who would be there for her each morning and every night and for all of her tomorrows. Not some danger junkie on the four-to-midnight shift who was married to his job.

"All done," he said hoarsely, but he couldn't seem to make his stupid body move away from her.

"No, we're not."

She pushed the bathroom door closed with her foot. The latch clicked. He made the mistake of looking into her eyes, and they were soft and glowing.

"You promised to take care of me," she whispered, and licked into his mouth.

He couldn't stand it. He kissed her back, using his teeth and his tongue, and instead of saying "ouch" or "stop it" or "I am not that kind of girl," she clenched her hand in his hair and totally blew his control.

He grabbed her hips and slid her forward across the cold, smooth top of the toilet to pull her against him, hard. Her encouraging moan was muffled by his mouth. They grappled and clutched, breathing wildly, kissing furiously. She wrapped her legs around his waist and he heard a thump. He went on kissing her, greedy for the taste of her, drowning in the scent of her, flowers and Faye, and it was only when he felt something soak the knees of his jeans that he realized she'd kicked the shampoo bottle off the edge of the tub.

He swore.

She giggled.

"Hang on," he said desperately. "Just let me—"

He levered himself to his feet and lifted her. She clung to his shoulders, his neck. He reached under her skirt to get his hands on her tight little butt, and her heels bumped the wall. His fingers dug into her—she was smooth and hot, and he wanted her bad—as he fumbled with the knob and maneuvered them through the door.

She nipped his chin, and he nearly stumbled.

"Bed," he said succinctly. "Room."

That was important, taking her to a bed, although for the life of him at this moment he couldn't remember why.

The door to her room was open. Another time, he'd like to explore the puzzle of her, get to know her through her possessions, her photographs, her hairbrush, the book beside her bed, but all he really cared about now was the bed itself. The bright print sheets beckoned him, inviting as an unlocked window to a burglar.

Faye's hands tightened convulsively on his shoulders. He kicked the door closed behind them, dropped her on the mattress and came down on top of her.

After that, it was all speed and heat and delight as they wrestled and rolled. He got his shirt off, and hers. He sucked in his breath at the sight of her, pale and perfect, her pink-tipped breasts tight with desire. He feasted on them, making himself crazy, making her moan.

He grappled with his belt buckle and she sat up, nearly clipping his jaw with the top of her head.

"Wait," she gasped. "I bought condoms."

He could have kissed her for her foresight. Only if he kissed her right then, he wasn't sure he would last long enough to take care of birth control.

"Where?" he asked.

"In the bag. From the drugstore. You have it, don't you?"

Sort of. He remembered dropping both bags by her worktable.

"I'll get it," he promised.

He left her warm and half-naked on her bed—*hurry,* his body urged—and charged toward the living room. The pearl gray twilight barely penetrated the long windows. He flicked on a lamp. *Hurry.*

There. Two bags, white rectangles in the dark, balanced against the table leg.

He snatched them up and turned off the light and tried to make it back to the bedroom and Faye without stumbling into something and waking—

Jamal.

Aleksy froze in the hallway.

His heart pounded. There wasn't a sound from the kid's room.

Relief loosened Aleksy's shoulders. How did parents with children do it?

He would have to ask Jarek, he decided, and didn't pause to examine why he thought that would be necessary. *Hurry, hurry.*

He opened the door to Faye's bedroom. She was still there, waiting for him, her slim white shoulders rising above the purple-and-green sheets and her breasts and thighs making scenic detours in the landscape of the bed.

There was a god, and he had just answered all of Aleksy's prayers.

He locked the door behind him.

Faye switched on the bedside lamp. Her cap of gold

hair gleamed in the yellow light. Her eyes were dark and welcoming.

"Did you find them?" she asked.

Momentarily deprived of speech, he held up the bags in answer.

She smiled, and his heart stopped. "Hurry."

Oh, yeah. Need pumped through him.

But something—the delay, maybe, or the reminder of the teenager sleeping across the hall or the delicacy of Faye's features shining in the lamplight—had blunted the edge of his urgency.

It wasn't that he wanted her any less. No. He wanted more. More time to look, to touch, to linger. To trace her slight curves and smooth planes with his hands and lips. To savor the textures and the tastes of her.

More time. More tenderness.

For the first time, he wanted both. The realization fought its way to the surface of his mind like a drowning swimmer. He wanted—

"Aleksy?" Faye shifted under the sheet, and his thoughts sank, swamped by desire. "Is anything wrong?"

He shook his head. Found his voice. "Nope."

"Then what are you doing standing over there?"

"I was just noticing how beautiful you are," he told her honestly.

She blushed, the color staining her baby fine skin. He really liked that he could make her blush with something as simple as a compliment. Maybe that was something else he could give her more of.

"I like your eyes," he said.

"They're brown."

He frowned. Okay. Either she was feeling insecure,

or she thought he was insincere. Neither possibility sat well with him.

The memory of her words challenged him. *I thought you didn't use my name because it saved you the trouble of remembering who was under you.*

"I know what color your eyes are," he said, "And I remember your name. For the record, I know exactly who I'm about to make love to and there's not another woman in the world I'd rather be with."

Her fingers tightened on the sheet. "In that case…"

Hope pressed like a weight on his chest.

"In that case, what?" he asked truculently.

She lifted a corner of the covers. "Maybe you better come to bed."

Aleksy grinned. "You bet. Right away."

Chapter 14

Faye arched against the sheets.

No one died of pleasure. In her mind, she knew that.

But her body, oh, her body quivered like a harp string, vibrating with the lovely music Aleksy's mouth and hands created in her. He stroked her and made her hum, plucked at her and forced a gasp to the back of her throat.

She expected heat. She was ready for sex. She thought she knew him and the fierce satisfaction of his possession.

But nothing had prepared her for the devastating force of Aleksy's slow seduction.

He suckled her breasts to aching peaks, soothed and aroused them with his tongue. His hands skimmed her, lightly, gently, as he brought his mouth back to hers, as he stole her breath and emptied her mind with more slow, drugging kisses.

She stretched to evade him, struggled to survive him. "What happened to 'right away'?" she asked.

"Later," he said.

And his busy mouth moved down again, sliding over her breasts, gliding along her shivering torso. His hair brushed her belly. His head was dark between her thighs.

Restless, embarrassed, she tried to bring her knees together, but he held her open with his hands, held her captive with his hot gaze.

How could what he did to her in the privacy of her room feel more daring, more dangerous, than sex under the stars?

But her heart trembled.

She licked her lips. "You don't need to—"

"Oh, yeah," he said softly, still holding her gaze. "I do."

He lowered his head. He nipped and licked, laved and sucked, drenched her with sensation and destroyed her with sweetness.

She would shatter if he didn't stop.

She would die if he did.

Self-preservation demanded she keep her mind above the dark tide surging through her body.

But when he rose above her, sweat gleaming on his face and damp on the back of his neck, she strained off the mattress to meet him. His dark gaze fixed on hers, too beautiful to bear. Linked with her, hand to hand and heat to heat, he plunged into her, joined with her and moved. His body pounded hers, came into hers, again and again, and she was swept away.

Like a suicide going into the surf, she gave up the struggle, yielded her body and surrendered her heart.

* * *

They curled, spoon fashion, in Faye's bed. Aleksy was warm and heavy behind her. As she stirred, his arms tightened around her waist and he pressed a kiss to her eyebrow.

"How are you feeling?" he asked huskily.

Terrified, she thought.

"Fine," she said.

She turned cautiously against his body, searching his face for clues. How was she supposed to feel, think, behave, now that she'd realized she was fathoms deep in love with him?

"And you?"

His grin flashed. "Never better."

Oh. Well, that was good. Wasn't it? Her total capitulation made him happy.

No, that was unfair, she chided herself. *She* wasn't being fair. Aleksy hadn't asked for her heart. And she would not ask for his love.

She knew the reasons he was here. He was paying a debt to a former girlfriend and satisfying his own exacting sense of responsibility. Faye didn't even enter into the equation.

No, that wasn't entirely accurate. *I moved in figuring I could stake out my suspect and maybe get laid at the same time.*

Somewhere along the line, she thought—she hoped—Aleksy had come to want something more. But she wouldn't make the mistake of thinking his basic character had changed.

What had he said about his murdered partner? *She wanted more than I could give. To her or any woman.*

Faye was pretty sure that included twenty-five-year-old art teachers with conveniently located cottages.

So if all he could give her was his wicked sense of

humor and practical support, his stubborn protection and bone-melting sex, well, that would have to be enough.

She would make it be enough.

Aleksy rolled away from her, depriving her of his warmth, and sat on the edge of the mattress. "You want anything?"

Yes.

Love.

Promises.

A future.

The fierceness of her response tore through her pretense of acceptance like a palette knife through wet paper.

"What did you have in mind?" she asked carefully.

"Something to eat?"

She narrowed her eyes. "You want me to cook for you?"

"No. Well, unless you want to. Especially if you don't put any clothes on first." He leered. "The idea of you naked in the kitchen definitely appeals to me. But given that we have a teenager in the house, that little scenario may have to wait. How about I fix us both a sandwich?"

She was caught considering the implications of sharing a house and a kitchen at some future date. Was he serious? And how could she possibly think about food?

"I'm not really hungry," she said.

"I am. Starved. Mind if I...?"

She propped her back against the headboard, anchoring the sheet across her breasts with her upper arms. "Be my guest," she invited wryly.

Aleksy reached for his pants. He intended to be a hell of a lot more to her than that.

Maybe she didn't get that yet—her loser parents had obviously done a real number on her when it came to understanding what she deserved and had a right to— but he was willing to work on it.

She was in his head. Under his skin. Part of him. His.

And as soon as he refueled, he would show her all over again.

Anticipation buzzed pleasantly through his veins. Zipping his jeans, he bent to kiss her briefly on her soft, warm mouth.

"Be right back," he promised.

She regarded him quizzically, her hair bright against the dark wood of the bed. "I'm not going anywhere."

They would have to talk about that, too, Aleksy thought as he strode barefoot down the hall. Women always needed to talk, and Faye, while extraordinary, was probably no exception.

Sometime—*later,* after he made love to her again— they would have a nice long talk about why she couldn't stay in Eden.

He rummaged in the refrigerator for cold cuts and mustard. Faye would understand he couldn't afford a distraction right now. He couldn't bear it if anything happened to her.

He snagged a plastic sleeve of bread from the pantry. She and Jamal would go back to Chicago, and after he wrapped up the investigation here, he would join them.

Or maybe Faye would want to move back up here for a while, Aleksy mused, piling ham and cheese on a slice of bread. The commute would be a bitch for him, of course, but there was something appealing about finishing the summer here in Eden, where it all began.

He was whistling as he loaded his sandwich onto a plate and carried it into the living room.

Almost out of habit, he glanced through the sliding doors and across the dark inlet.

And his appetite died.

You can't run away from your problems, Faye had told Jamal only this morning. You have to face them.

So she sat with the sheet tucked under her arms, every muscle nearly weeping in gratitude, and faced her feelings squarely.

She was in love. All the way, head over heels in love with Aleksy Denko.

She drew a tight breath. This was a problem.

She understood, she truly did, that he wasn't ready to make a commitment outside of his job. All right. She accepted that. That didn't mean they couldn't—

The door banged open.

Aleksy sat on the end of the bed, depressing the mattress under him, and began to lace up his boots.

No amount of understanding had prepared her for this.

"What are you doing?"

He glanced at her over his shoulder, his face hard, his eyes dark and distracted. "I have to go out."

She hitched the sheet higher over her breasts. "When will you be back?"

"I don't know." He stood. "Can I borrow your camera?"

"I—I guess so. Yes."

"Thanks." Bare-chested, he began to leave the room.

Her heart beat like a rabbit's, fast and frightened. "Where are you going?"

He looked at her as if he'd forgotten who she was. Maybe, for a moment, he had. "I have to get a sweater," he explained.

And his gun, she thought. Of course he would need his gun.

He was gone before the sheets beside her had completely cooled.

There was a difference between quitting and being defeated, she'd said to Jamal.

Defeated, she covered her face with her hands and wept.

Faye drifted like a ghost through her own living room, her chest hollowed out and her throat achy.

When he came back, she thought, they would talk. In the meantime, she would keep moving. Keep busy. She could transfer Jamal's laundry to the dryer. She would straighten the living room. She could…

Wait.

She turned on a lamp at the corner of the couch. The light pooled on an uneaten ham sandwich, mute evidence of Aleksy's desertion.

She closed her eyes. How did Tess stand it? she wondered. How would she?

Where was Aleksy now? She was sure his disappearance had something to do with the case. With Richard Freer.

Old white guys with guns make me nervous.

She carried the plate into the kitchen and covered it with plastic wrap. Aleksy would be back. He had to come back. For his sandwich. She put it in the fridge.

Hugging her elbows, she wandered back to the cottage's main room, avoiding the temptation of the long windows. The Irish in her made her superstitious. As long as she didn't look, her attention couldn't draw other watchful eyes in the night to search for Aleksy.

She bit her lip. Oh, God, she was losing her mind.

She emptied the jar of paint-tinged water on her worktable. She dug one of her sandals from under the couch. She plucked the white Weiglund's Camera bag from the floor.

Idly she broke the adhesive seal. Casually she slipped the photos from the envelope. The most recent ones were on top: six different camera angles of the wood pile by the house and a breathtaking shot of the sunset that completely failed to capture the colors she remembered. She'd never make a photographer. Frowning, she thumbed through the stack.

And there, from the beginning of the roll, were two developed prints of a beige midsize cabin cruiser riding the coral lake at dawn.

Her heart pounded. The first wide shot showed the sag of the dock and the angles of the boathouse behind the sport cabin. And the other—the hand holding the pictures trembled—the other, taken with the zoom, showed a tiny string of numbers printed just below the cabin's flat black window. The registration number. She had to tell Aleksy.

Aleksy wasn't here.

She forced herself to breathe. To think.

She could tell Jarek. Jarek would know what to do.

She wasted seconds wondering how she could get the police chief's home number. Stupid. She could just call 911.

She left her name and number with the pleasant-voiced dispatcher and waited in an agony of impatience by the phone.

When it rang, she jumped. "Hello?"

"Faye, it's Jarek Denko." The police chief's voice was reassuringly official. "What can I do for you?"

"I found another photograph," she blurted. "Of the boat. I just had it developed."

He didn't ask which boat. He said, "Does Aleksy know?"

"He's not here. He went out. In a hurry."

The receiver in her hand was silent as Jarek put the two pieces of information together.

With nothing to do but think for long, anxious minutes, Faye had run some mental calculations of her own. "Was that—could that be why my purse was snatched this afternoon?"

"Could be," Jarek said slowly. Calmly. "Did anyone know you had the pictures with you?"

"I was holding the bag from the camera shop. When we walked down the street." She swallowed. "We stopped at Liberty Sporting Goods. Someone—" Richard Freer, she meant "—could have seen."

"How clear is the picture?" His voice was sharp now.

"Pretty clear. I had my zoom."

"Can you read the registration number?"

Her palms were damp. "I think so. There's a 2, and then a 3 or an 8, another 3 or an 8, and then a 5."

He repeated the numbers back to her. She confirmed them.

He didn't say anything.

"What?" she demanded, and then bit her tongue.

"I'm just running that number through the—" He broke off.

Her stomach contracted into a tight little ball. "Jarek?"

"Did Aleksy say why he went out?"

Oh, God. "No."

"The boat," Jarek said. "This is a long shot, but— is it there now?"

She hadn't looked. She hadn't thought to look. Or she'd been afraid to.

Clutching the receiver, she scrambled to the window.

"It's dark. It's half a mile to Freer's dock and the security lights aren't on."

Why, she wondered frantically, would Freer turn out his lights?

"Faye." Jarek's voice was hard as January ice. "Can you see the dock at all? How many boats are there?"

"I don't—" She strained to see through the dark. The quarter moon shed petals of light on the water but barely disturbed the shadows on the opposite shore. "Two, I guess. Three?"

"Two, or three?"

"I can't tell. Maybe three."

"Okay," Jarek said. "If that boat matches the registration number you just gave me, we've got our probable cause. Give me twenty minutes to get a warrant, and I'll be there to check things out. You stay put."

Staying put was good, Faye told herself, hanging up the phone.

She wasn't Dick Tracy.

She wasn't even Nancy Drew.

She didn't want to get involved.

Shivering, she stared out at the gleaming water and the dim, indistinct bank. The drone of unidentified insects—crickets? water bugs?—created a curtain of sound. Frogs sang in cadence.

Until a shot cracked over the water, shattering the night.

Aleksy hadn't spent so much time crouching in bushes since he and Jarek used to play war with the

Dolan brothers at Indian Boundary Park. His heart still thumped. His boots still got muddy. And no matter how carefully he scouted the ground beforehand, he still wound up with a rock jabbing his knee and twigs sticking the back of his neck.

He had a good view of the dock, though.

Three boats.

Including a pale tan Parker Pilothouse with a Yamaha outboard engine and no one on board.

The tinted glass made it difficult to see inside but it was dark enough that anybody on that boat would need a light. No light shone in the cabin. No light shone on the deck. Therefore nobody was home. Which suited Aleksy just fine.

He crawled from his bush into the shadow of the boathouse, Faye's camera bumping his chest, feeling as if at any moment Tommy Dolan was going to leap out of hiding and pound him to the ground. Nothing. No Tommy. No Dick or Harry, either. Richard Freer and his nameless, faceless guest stayed conveniently out of the way at the house.

The grassy bank was gray in the moonlight. Aleksy crossed to the dock, stopped and listened. More nothing. Just the chorus of slimy night life, the slap of the water and the rasp of his own breathing.

Neither of Freer's boats—an open console motorboat and a flat sailboat, low on the water—provided much cover as he picked his way along the dock. But that was okay. A few more yards and he stood beside the pilothouse.

Supporting himself with one hand on a piling, he stepped cautiously over the side and onto the deck. It rocked and shifted underfoot and he nearly lost his bal-

ance. He was a street cop, not a damn Coast Guard
patrol. He couldn't navigate, couldn't steer, could
barely walk upright without slipping.

But he did know how to conduct a search.

The pilothouse door had a standard lock, easy to
monkey. Aleksy was grateful. He didn't mind a little
B & E, but he didn't want to leave signs he'd been
there. A switch activated the dome light overhead. He
left it alone, turning on the tiny desk lamp clamped to
the left of the console instead. In the dim light, he surveyed the cabin.

He didn't have a clue what all those gauges and dials
were for, but the setup sure looked high-tech. His blood
hummed. There was a PC flush mounted into the console, more than any Sunday fisherman would need. He
took the lens cap off Faye's camera, set it to imprint
with the date and time, and lifted the flash bar to take
a picture. Several pictures, standing with his back to the
tinted windows to minimize the flash.

A tiny access door led to the forward cabin. He tried
it. Locked. And not with any sissy lock, either. Whatever proof he needed, whatever arsenal Freer had
amassed for illegal sale to Amir, was probably stored
below. But he took another minute to search the pilothouse, opening drawers, reaching under the console.
Working vice had taught him how to find the things
most people wanted to hide.

Bingo.

His heart pumped in excitement. In the cushioned
seat box to the left of the door was a fifty shot Calico
semiautomatic carbine rifle—legal, if purchased legally
in the United States. It would be interesting to see what
the ATF would turn up on a firearms trace.

And in a sliding drawer under the dash, within easy

reach of the pilot, along with the usual fishing boat junk, hooks and wire and flashlight batteries, were two pineapple style military hand grenades.

Aleksy grinned a wolf's grin. Illegal possession of destructive devices. Hot damn.

He adjusted the lens and took more pictures. You didn't go fishing with those suckers. Unless you liked your catch belly up and by the hundreds.

He stepped back to get a wider console shot, with the open drawer and the grenades nestled inside. A videotape would have been even better, but he figured he had enough evidence here to send the right guys after Karen's killers.

This one's for you, partner.

A rifle barked. The window cracked. Something smacked into the console.

The night erupted in a flash of light and pain, and Aleksy dropped to the cabin floor.

"No way." Jamal shifted to block the door. The teenager was clearly uncomfortable. His voice was embarrassed. His eyes were miserable.

But his stance—Faye's heart sank—his stance was determined.

"Sorry, Harp," he mumbled. "But I can't let you go out there."

"Jamal, I am an adult. You can't stop me."

This was so patently untrue that the boy didn't even bother to contradict her. He looked at her, then away, and shuffled his feet.

Faye changed tactics. "I'll be fine."

"Weren't no car backfire that woke me up," Jamal said. "Whoever is out there has got a gun."

Nerves jittered in her stomach. "No one's going to shoot at me," she said.

Who was she trying to reassure? Jamal? Or herself?

Jamal shook his head. "Anybody dumb enough to mess with Denko would shoot you as soon as look at you."

"I'm not a threat to them."

The teenager raised his eyebrows. "You know who they are?"

"I—" For the first time, she sympathized with Aleksy's determination to keep her in protected ignorance. "It's a police matter," she said.

"Then let the police handle it."

"I called the police. They're on the way."

"What do you need to go out there for, then?"

I am practicing facing my fears. I'm afraid that the noble, thickheaded adrenaline junkie I'm in love with could be out there bleeding to death.

"Chief Denko said it would take him twenty minutes to get here. That might be too late."

"You mean, like, if he's been shot."

She winced. It sounded so melodramatic. "Yes."

"You know where he is?"

"I can guess."

"And you think you can get to him before the police? And before whatever bad guys are out there find him and finish him off?"

Uncertainty shook her. She said, honestly, "I don't know. All I know is I'll never forgive myself if I don't try. At the very least, maybe I can provide a distraction until—until the police arrive."

"You mean, a target," he said in disgust. "Damn. Okay. I'll go with you."

"No," she objected instinctively. "It's not—"

He waited for her to say it. *It's not safe.*

She sighed. "What will you say if we're caught?"

Jamal hunched his shoulders. "What would you say?"

"It doesn't matter what I say. I'm not a threat," she repeated and heard the teasing echo of Aleksy's voice. *You're a cream puff.* "I'll claim I heard a noise and needed a big, strong man to protect me."

"Yeah, well, that's why you got me along," Jamal said.

Gratitude warred with doubt. She should argue with him. She should make him stay. But debating would only prolong her uncertainty. She needed to know if Aleksy was all right. And if he wasn't—if he was lying somewhere, hiding, bleeding, alone—then she needed to find him.

"We'll take my car," she decided. "It's almost two miles around by road. And when we get there, you stay in the car, understand? I don't want anyone to see you."

"They won't spot me." The teenager grinned crookedly. "I'm harder to see in the dark than you are."

Chapter 15

He had to get up.

Get moving.

Fast.

Dizzied, deafened and almost blind, Aleksy squinted at the splintered pattern in the safety glass, glittering like a spiderweb in the moonlight.

He was lucky they hadn't blown away the top of his skull. The ricochet had ploughed through his scalp instead, thanks to the darkness, the distorting glass and the rocking boat. But the constant stream of blood into his eyes was annoying.

Not to mention that it hurt like a son of a bitch.

He'd hurt a lot worse if he didn't get his butt out of here. He started to crawl. Around the pedestal pilot's chair, across the cabin floor. At the door, he listened, blinking away blood. No shouts, no footsteps. Good or bad? he wondered.

He pulled himself up the step and through the door onto the deck of the cockpit.

The security lights snapped on, flooding the bank. Shadows jumped on the deck.

He rolled into the narrow darkness cast by the side of the boat, his heart thudding, his blood pumping over his forehead and into his eyes.

Somebody had decided they wanted to find him more than they wanted to minimize the presence of the boat. Which meant they wanted him. Bad. Maybe dead. Hell.

Your move, hotshot.

He could hear footsteps now. Running.

Move fast.

He put his hands on the side, pulled up and swung a leg over. The movement made him dizzy. Sick. He lay flat along the side a moment, fighting nausea and gravity. He couldn't splash. He must not make a splash. Reversing his grip, he took a deep breath and lowered himself over the side, into the water.

The camera scraped the side of the boat before it bumped below the surface. The film could be salvaged by a knowledgeable developer, but the camera would be ruined. Damn. He was going to owe Faye a new one.

He owed her a lot of things, but he had to pay his debts in order. Justice for Karen, and then…

First he had to stay alive.

His boots filled until they felt like ten-pound weights at the end of his ankles. He released his hold and went down, water filling his ears and nostrils, pain seeping, eating along his wound. He bit back a gasp, fought not to kick, struggled not to make a sound.

Blind and breathless, he blundered into a piling. His hands patted and groped at the slick surface before he found a hold and pulled himself up.

Warm blood and cold water streamed over his face. Blink. Breathe. He tasted salt and silt and gasoline. He was under the dock. Okay.

Footsteps thumped down the dock. They sure as hell weren't trying to hide from him. He edged around the piling, deeper into the black, weedy shadows. He needed to get out, get away. He hugged the piling, held his breath, as his pursuers—pursuer, he only heard one set of feet overhead—moved toward the boat.

He still had his gun. Although getting a drop in the dark on a mope with a rifle while he was three-quarters drowned and bleeding profusely from a bullet wound in the head... Yeah. Not a good idea.

If he could get to the bank...

To the bushes...

To his car...

"Make sure you got him," Freer called from the shore.

At least two of them, then. One on the boat and one on the bank.

And he was trapped between.

Faye slowed her car as she reached the bottom of the winding drive that led to Richard Freer's half-million-dollar home. Her headlights sprang off the black-and-orange signs posted in the woods on either side.

Private Property, they read. Keep Out.

At least they didn't say, Trespassers Will Be Shot.

She searched for a clear stretch of shoulder to leave the car.

There wasn't one. Apparently Richard didn't believe in encouraging day-trippers and weekend fishermen to park along his piece of road.

She spotted a stand of taller bushes, impenetrable in

the dark. Perhaps only in contrast, the trees around them seemed thinner. She edged her car forward, following the beam of her headlights, and found a bumpy passage off road, through the leaves and underbrush.

And Aleksy's TransAm, low slung and gleaming, blacker than the night.

Relief and triumph made her dizzy. She was already sitting, so she put her head down on the steering wheel and concentrated on taking deep breaths.

"Harp?" Jamal sounded anxious. "You okay?"

She couldn't lose it now. She wasn't defeated yet. She was on the right track. And she had a seventeen-year-old amphetamine junkie and a thirty-three-year-old cop possibly bleeding to death from a gunshot wound both depending on her.

She raised her head and forced a smile. It probably wasn't a very convincing smile, but maybe it was dark enough that Jamal would be fooled.

"I'm fine," she said. "He was here, see? That's his car."

In the dim glow of the dash, Jamal looked unimpressed. "Swell. What do we do now?"

Good question.

"I'm going to see if he's inside—" slumped, bleeding, unconscious, *oh, God* "—and you're going to stay in the car."

"Uh-uh. It's creepy here."

The woods were dense and dark and alive with sounds—trembling leaves and mindless insects, scuttling forest creatures and the predators that hunt the night.

To a city kid it probably was creepy. Despite her summer visits to her aunt, Faye felt a little creeped herself.

She fought to sound in control. "Tough it out," she said.

Jamal made a disgusted sound—she couldn't see if he rolled his eyes or not—and slouched in his seat.

Faye grabbed the flashlight her aunt always kept in the kitchen drawer for emergencies—although Eileen had to have been thinking floods and ice storms, not gunrunners and midnight searches—turned off the car and swung open her door. It crunched into a bush. That was okay. She got out, trying hard not to think about poison ivy.

"Watch out for snakes," Jamal said.

Snakes? Her heart leapt into her throat. The flashlight beam jumped off the hood of the TransAm before she tightened her grip. She had bigger worries. Like whether she was going to have any chance at all to fight for a future with Aleksy or whether he was out there somewhere bleeding himself into an early grave.

She picked her way to the dark sports car and tried the door. It was locked. She shone her flashlight through the window. Empty.

Her heart still hadn't settled from the snake threat. She played the light again over Aleksy's upholstery, as if he would magically turn up tucked between the cushions like lost change.

He didn't.

Indecision made her hand waver. What now? She could hardly go bang on Richard Freer's door and demand that the gun dealer produce Aleksy.

Leaves crackled behind her.

She turned to order Jamal back into the car, but it wasn't Jamal's voice that carried through the dark and froze her blood.

"Faye. I'm sorry to find you mixed up in this." Richard Freer sounded genuinely disappointed. "Not surprised, not really, but so sorry."

Her mouth went dry. She started to shake, standing beside Aleksy's empty car armed with nothing but a flashlight.

Watch out for snakes.

Freer was gone.

That was the good news.

The bad news was before Freer left he had a nice long talk with Mr. Rifle on the dock. The shooter was now patrolling the lit bank with his gun pointed casually at the water. If any vacationers in this exclusive, secluded neighborhood happened to be out on their balconies with binoculars at eleven o'clock at night, all they would see was a solitary sportsman with an expensive rifle scope out gunning for bluegill in the dark.

Aleksy certainly *hoped* that would prompt a call to the police. He'd be mighty happy to see Jarek drive up right now. But he couldn't count on it.

He had to get out of this one on his own.

He lay on his stomach at the edge of the light, half hidden by the bushes overgrowing the bank, half submerged in brackish water. Never mind that he was better at negotiating dark alleys than muddy banks. Never mind that his clothes were soaked, his boots weighed fifteen pounds apiece, and he shook from cold and shock. Never mind that his scalp was on fire and the gore of his wound had attracted a tormenting swarm of midges and mosquitoes.

The bleeding had slowed.

Freer had left.

It was time to roll.

The shooter strolled within yards of his hiding place.

He was a dark, ordinary-looking guy in dark, ordinary clothes. He wore a charcoal ball cap with the brim pulled low.

How had Faye described her attacker? *Dark pants, navy shirt and a—gray?—ball cap. Very ordinary, really.*

In the shadows, Aleksy's eyes narrowed. His lip pulled back from his teeth. This bastard had had his hands on Faye, had pushed her down and hurt her. He owed him. Big time.

But not yet.

Aleksy couldn't risk screwing up his chance to nail Freer.

When the shooter turned and patrolled back toward the dock, Aleksy slithered on his elbows up the bank and crawled into the screening bushes.

Faye swung the flashlight in the direction of Richard's voice. The beam painted an arc on the surrounding trees, jumped off his white face, and wavered on the snub, black gun in his hand.

Immediately a bright light hit her own eyes, blinding her.

"Turn it off, Faye. I think one light is all we need. We don't want accidents."

Fear stuck in her throat. She swallowed hard and complied.

"Who are you with?" Freer inquired. "ATF? FBI?"

If she wasn't a threat, Faye thought frantically, he wouldn't shoot her. She could not give him any cause to consider her a threat.

Which was fine by her, because at this moment, with her knees quaking and her mouth parched with terror, she felt about as threatening as Jell-O.

She worked enough saliva to her tongue to say, "I don't know what you're talking about. I'm not with anybody. I'm here alone."

She didn't dare glance behind her. Surely, even in the woods, Jamal had the street smarts to lay low and stay put?

"Are you trying to tell me that's not your boyfriend's car?" Richard asked.

"My—well, yes. We had a fight." She didn't have to pretend the distress that shook her voice. "He said things, I said things... You know how it is. Anyway, he took off, and after a while I got worried about him. Have you seen him?" she asked eagerly, as an afterthought.

"I think so," Richard said. "He was down on my dock. On one of my boats, in fact."

Oh, dear.

"You must be mistaken," Faye said. "Alex isn't even interested in boats."

"No? Then maybe his real interest is what I had on board."

Her stomach dropped in dread and dismay. Richard was too suspicious. She couldn't pretend innocence much longer.

"I'm sorry if Alex was trespassing," she said politely. "I guess he wasn't thinking clearly. I mean, we had this fight—"

"Don't you want to know what I have on board?"

"Not really," she said. "I mean, it's none of my business, is it?"

"It's a shame, then, that your boyfriend got you involved. Guns, Faye," Richard said gently, as if explaining things to a not particularly bright student. "I had guns on board."

She blinked. "Well, of course you have guns. You're a gun dealer, aren't you?"

He laughed. "You're really very good. I hope your boyfriend appreciates you enough to make a deal."

The flashlight beam got brighter and wider as he approached. Her hands were shaking. Her heart was cold, and her brain froze so that she couldn't think.

"What do you mean?" she said, and it was no effort at all to sound lost and confused.

Richard reached out and grabbed her wrist. In a smooth, brutal move, he twisted her arm behind her and pressed the muzzle of the gun under her jaw.

"Let's see if we can find Alex," he suggested. "I'm interested to know what he's willing to trade for your life."

Aleksy had been a Boy Scout. He knew how to tie knots, splint a snakebite and make fire.

All of which qualified him to be a contestant on one of those TV survival shows but was no damn good at all when it came to stealing silently through the woods in wet boots with a broken camera around his neck and a bleeding head wound.

Unless, of course, he got bit by a snake.

The woods were even darker than the water. He tried to stick close to the road, where the pale light of the new moon slanted through the trees, but he couldn't risk running into Freer or his trigger-happy accomplice. Better to get clean away with the evidence and call for backup from his car.

His vision blurred. His heart labored. His breathing rasped. Too loud. He swiped his forearm over his eyes and nearly doubled over from the pain. What the—?

His sweater. He must have caught the edge of the graze with his sweater. He wouldn't do it again.

He hugged a tree trunk—plenty of those around—and took deep breaths until the world stopped spinning.

Setting his jaw, he staggered on, trying to place his feet with care, even though the ground jumped and slid before him like an outtake from the *Blair Witch Project*.

Something crashed through the trees on his left, going down to the water.

Deer?

No deer was ever that loud.

And then he stopped caring because he heard voices coming from the private road.

Freer's voice. He was pretty sure he recognized that. And Faye's.

His blood ran cold.

"—making a terrible mistake," Faye protested, her voice breathy. Bewildered. "I'm just an art teacher. You could call my school—well, not now, but in the morning—and—"

"Honey, by morning I'm not going to care what you do."

Hot rage erupted in Aleksy, drumming in his head like blood, so that he lost the first few words of Faye's reply.

"—for the offer, but I'm already in a relationship."

"Are you? Did you know he was only using you to spy on me? Or don't you care?"

Aleksy started moving toward the road as quietly as he could, as quickly as he dared.

"I don't know what you're talking about," Faye said. "Alex loves me."

The simple faith in her voice almost tripped him up. She was a really good actress. Had to be. Because if she believed that... If he believed her... Damn it, he couldn't deal with this right now. A hostage situation was no time to think about till-death-do-us-part.

"You better hope so," Freer said. "Or you'll be dead by morning."

Aleksy drew his gun from the small of his back. He saw them now, through the trees, Freer and Faye walking close together in the uncertain moonlight like a parody of lovers. The bastard had her arm twisted behind her and the barrel of his gun pressed under her delicate jaw.

Aleksy cursed silently, steadily.

Shoot/Don't shoot. The kind of situation every cop was trained to evaluate and decide.

He was a good shot. Not SWAT team caliber, maybe, but he practiced regularly at the range. "Hotshot," Jarek had dubbed him when, as a cocky rookie, he'd first followed his brother on to the force. The name had stuck. He was good.

He raised his weapon and sighted down the short barrel at Freer's head. Not the body. The risk of hitting Faye was too great.

Shoot.

He blinked. His vision still hadn't cleared. The angle was bad. The light was worse. His head throbbed and his hand shook.

Don't shoot.

Freer shoved Faye forward. "You know, you could save us some time if you screamed. Get his attention."

Faye's chin raised. Maybe she was only trying to avoid the barrel of the gun. But she said, quite clearly, "Go to hell."

Freer yanked upward on her captive arm and she made a soft, distressed sound.

Aleksy's muscles tightened. *Shoot.*

But he had to get in front of them first. He picked and pushed a path as silently as he could, sweat running down his spine, blood crawling down his face.

The road they were on was smoother and more direct than the track through the trees, but Faye hampered Freer's progress. She hung against him, not quite struggling, but making him work for every step.

Smart girl, Aleksy thought. Smart, brave girl. If they both lived through this, he was going to marry her.

They were getting closer to the house. Aleksy could see the flat, silver gleam of the lake through the trees. They would meet up with the shooter soon.

It had to be now.

He raised his chief's special in hands that trembled slightly, only slightly, from cold and shock.

He couldn't do it. This wasn't a paper target he was taking aim at. It was a man who quite literally held Faye's life in his hands—hands already stained with Karen's blood.

Aleksy shut down his emotions, turned off his rioting thoughts, made himself like the gun in his hand, a cold, well-oiled machine focused on one thing.

Faye.

Don't shoot.

He closed his eyes again. He could do this. All he needed was one shot. One clear shot. Or a miracle.

But when he opened his eyes, there was no miracle. No flashing lights or screeching sirens. No cavalry or brother riding to the rescue. No help. No hope.

Only footsteps scuffing up the road from the direction of the lake. The shooter.

It couldn't get much worse than this.

Only it did.

"Any sign?" Freer asked the newcomer.

"No one. No body. I think he is alive."

"Don't look so happy, honey," Freer advised. "Your boyfriend just abandoned you."

"I'll survive," she told him. No trace of the cream puff at all.

"Will you?" Freer traced the gun down the side of her throat. She strained her head away. Aleksy kept watching, looking, praying for the opportunity that didn't come. "Let's see if we can change his mind."

He was enjoying this, the bastard.

"How?" Faye asked, her voice remarkably steady.

"We're going to make you scream."

It wouldn't do any good to give himself up.

Aleksy knew that. In a hostage situation, the responding officer's first duty was to contain the suspects and maintain cover.

But what he knew and how he felt were two entirely different things. He shuddered with the effort to keep still, to stay hidden.

One clear shot, he promised himself. That's all he needed.

"I don't have time for this," the man with the rifle said, and some of the tension eased in Aleksy's gut. "I have to get my merchandise away."

"If my operation is shut down, there won't be any more merchandise," Freer said. "You'll need to find another licensed firearms buyer to make straw purchases for you."

Freer was convicting himself with every word. At the moment, it was hard to care.

The other man's gaze darted to Faye. He licked his lips. "You think this will bring the cop back?"

"Oh, yeah. If he's still around. If he isn't—" Freer

shrugged. ''At least we'll get a little something for our trouble.''

Faye struggled, but she did not make a sound.

Aleksy sighted along the blue steel barrel. He would kill him. Kill them both.

One clear shot, he prayed.

They ripped her blouse, Freer still holding her from behind, with the gun jammed into the tender joint of her head and throat.

Aleksy died inside.

Forget the miracle. He just needed a distraction.

And then the night exploded around them and the scene blasted apart. The explosion shook his bones and, for one startled moment, his concentration.

Faye.

Twenty yards away, water geysered, flame shot in a column, sparks flew. Wood and fiberglass were hurled into the air as the boat blew up out of the water.

Chapter 16

The guy with the rifle ran. Not away, which would have been sensible, but toward the explosion.

Hunting, Aleksy realized grimly. Hunting him.

It didn't matter. He had to save Faye.

Richard Freer whirled, spinning Faye in front of him. He raised his gun to answer this new threat, as if he expected demons to come boiling out of the inferno that had once been his dock.

One clear shot. Aleksy drew a deep breath, focusing his eyes, steadying his hand, shutting off his emotions.

Shoot.

He exhaled slowly. Squeezed the trigger gently.

The .38 kicked in his hand, its burst almost lost against the bombardment from the water. Pulse pounding, heart thumping, Aleksy watched Freer's arm, the arm supporting his gun, blossom with dark blood.

The dealer shrieked.

Faye squealed and doubled over. Aleksy's heart

stopped. Had he somehow hit her? Made Freer hit her? Was she hurt?

Not that hurt. She jabbed her elbow hard into Freer's stomach and twisted away.

Freer dropped to his knees. His uninjured arm made a surprising grab for her ankles that brought her down, hard. Her wrist crumpled as she tried to catch herself on the ground.

Son of a bitch.

Aleksy charged from the screen of trees, stumbling down the slight slope to the road, and launched himself at Freer's back.

With a satisfying woof, the man collapsed under him, the air driven from his lungs. Aleksy braced himself on his knees and wedged one hand between their bodies, fumbling to unbuckle his belt so he'd have something to tie the guy up with.

Freer reached back and grabbed Aleksy's hair, scratching the gash in his head.

For the second time, the world erupted in a blaze of stars. Pain. Nausea.

Fueled by adrenaline and desperation, Freer heaved and scrambled on top. He laced his fingers in Aleksy's hair. Pain, sickening, blinding, streaked through Aleksy's skull. Tightening his hold, Freer yanked Aleksy's head up and slammed it once, twice, three times on the hard dirt road.

Aleksy was losing it. Losing consciousness. Leaving Faye to face—what?—alone.

He had to fight. Had to—

Clumsily he wrenched his hand free and, more by luck and instinct than anything else, clamped it on Freer's bloody arm, dangling useless by his head.

Freer screamed and released him.

They rolled again while the night burned around them, Freer's contorted face diabolical in the flickering red glare.

"What can I do?" Faye's feet, in neat, flat sneakers, danced at the corner of his vision. Faye's voice, amazingly calm, drummed in his ears. "Tell me what to do."

"My...belt," Aleksy managed. Beneath him, Freer groaned and pitched. "Tie...him up."

He felt her small, urgent hands tugging at his waist. Freer strained and cursed. Aleksy struggled to hold his kicking legs while she wrapped his ankles with the belt and pulled the buckle tight.

"Now the arms," Aleksy instructed.

Faye hesitated. "What should I use?"

He grunted. "His belt."

"I can't reach his belt."

"Then use yours."

"I'm not wearing one."

"Okay."

Not okay. Aleksy tried to bend his mind around this new twist while Freer writhed under him and his thoughts fractured like a broken mirror.

"What about my bra?" Faye asked. "It's stretchy."

He was delirious. "What?"

But Faye had already turned her slim white back. Her bra straps dropped down her shoulders. She wriggled and tugged under her torn blouse and turned with her bra in her hands.

She knelt beside him. Clinging to consciousness, Aleksy shifted his weight.

Freer screamed when Faye moved his wounded arm. She froze, her brown eyes enormous in her white face.

The scene was fading in and out like a TV with bad reception. *He was losing it.*

"Do it," Aleksy commanded.

Somehow she got the job done. She rolled him away, onto his back, so she could test the elastic straps binding Freer's wrists and the thick leather around his ankles.

He lay flat while the earth tilted under him and the stars whirled overhead. His nausea returned. He closed his eyes.

Someone lifted his head—*Don't,* he wanted to yelp— and then something soft cradled it. Under the acrid burning, the blood and the mud, a nice, light fragrance wavered. Flowers. And Faye, he thought contentedly.

Funny that she should pick that moment to scream, a high, ululating wail that sounded exactly like—

"Sirens?" he asked, opening his eyes.

Faye nodded, her warm brown gaze concerned. "I called your brother. Before I left the cottage."

Of course she had. Smart, brave girl.

Grateful, reassured, he let himself slide into the darkness.

"Try not to worry," Tess said, handing Faye a foam cup of hospital coffee. "I told you cops have incredibly thick skulls."

Faye nodded. Sipped. Winced. This was worse than the brew in the teachers' lounge. Her stomach already churned from an uneasy blend of painkillers, reaction and fear. Adding coffee, bad coffee, to the mix was just too big a risk.

She set the cup on a waiting room table.

Tess must have observed the wince, because her full lips pursed in sympathy. "How's the wrist?"

Faye dragged her mind back from the memory of Aleksy's white, blood-streaked face and held up her newly bandaged wrist for inspection. "It's fine. I'm fine."

"You look whacked," Tess said frankly.

Beneath her skintight jeans and exotic good looks was a genuine maternal warmth that Faye found touching.

She felt bludgeoned by the events of the past twelve hours. She'd been knocked down, robbed and made love to. Two people she loved had been threatened. She had nearly been raped. Or worse. She'd been battered by fear, racked by uncertainty, manhandled by a well-dressed thug and thrown to the ground in the aftermath of an explosion.

"Whacked" summed up her feelings nicely.

But she was trying hard not to let it show.

She forced a smile. "I'm all right. Really."

"Just worried," Tess said.

It was a comfort to admit it. "Yes."

"It's tough, being in love with a cop."

Faye met Tess's understanding gaze. Another comfort. Another admission. "Yes."

The brunette sighed. "Look, it's none of my business, but he's not going to change."

It cost her, but Faye nodded again. In acceptance.

"No," she agreed softly. "I don't expect him to change."

The question was, could she?

Aleksy had warned her he wasn't the marrying kind. That the only person who could understand what being a cop was like was another cop.

Could she love him knowing she could lose him to the demands of his job or a bad guy's bullet? Knowing he would forever shut her out of that part of his life?

Could she take that risk?

Did she even have the choice anymore?

"Here's Jarek," Tess said. She hurried to her fiancé's side. "Did you see the doctor?"

"I did." He covered her hand where it rested on his arm and smiled over her head at Faye. "The CT scan showed no bleeding under the skull or in the brain tissue. His skull is fractured, and that graze in his head took thirty-two stitches to close, but Alex is going to be fine."

"Thank God," Tess breathed.

Yes. Thank God.

Faye sat, stunned with relief, absorbing the good news, letting it seep into every cell to heal her battered hopes and soothe her anxious heart.

He was going to be fine.

They were going to be—well, she didn't know if they were going to be fine or not. The realization caused a little tear in her heart.

"What about Jamal?" she asked.

Jarek raised his eyebrows at her apparent lack of response. "I just picked him up from the ER. You can ask him yourself," he said, and stepped aside.

The teenager swaggered through the doorway, soot stains on his clothes and a rakish bandage on his head.

"Hey, Harp," he greeted her.

"Jamal!"

She jumped up and grabbed him by both arms. "What happened? I told you to stay in the car!"

He rolled his eyes. "Oh, yeah, like I was going to sit tight while that Dick guy was threatening you."

"But what did you do?"

"I couldn't do anything at first, could I? Because the old guy is strapped and I'm not carrying. But I heard him tell you there were guns on his boat, see? So, once he gets you on the road, then I break through the woods to go get—"

The boy broke off to look at Jarek. "Do I want to be careful what I'm saying here?"

Jarek's light gray eyes gleamed with humor. "You went down to the dock to go get help," he suggested.

Jamal grinned. "Yeah. Like the man says, I'm looking for help. Only there's another guy with a gage down by the boats. So I wait until he leaves and I check out the boat."

"But…how did you know which boat to search?" Faye asked, bewildered.

Jamal shook his head with all the worldly disdain of a seventeen-year-old boy. "There was a bullet hole in the window, Harp."

Despite the horror of the night's events, Faye had to bite back a smile. "Yes, I can see that that would be a clue."

"Then you found a gun," Tess prompted.

He checked again with Jarek, who gave a slight nod.

"Yeah," said Jamal. "In one of those seat things, you know, that lifts up? Only it's, like, an AK-47 or something. No way am I going to be able to shoot that. So I'm looking around some more, and I got to tell you, I'm starting to sweat, because it's been a while since I left you with the Dick guy. And then—" He paused for emphasis, his dark eyes shining. "I found this grenade."

Faye felt faint. "A grenade."

Jamal beamed. "Yeah. It was so cool. Two of them, in a drawer."

"Oh, my God," Faye said. "You could have been killed."

Aleksy could have been killed. They all could have been blown to bits.

"No, Harp, it was okay. They've got those big circle things that you pull."

"Just like in the movies, he told me," Jarek murmured.

Jamal's head bobbed in agreement. "Yeah. Anyway, I knew you called Chief Denko, right? Only he hasn't shown and I'm thinking maybe he doesn't know where you are."

"We were Code Two—normal response, no lights or sirens," Jarek explained for Faye's benefit. "Plus, it took longer than I expected to find a magistrate for the search warrant."

"Which at the time I don't know," Jamal said. "So, I'm thinking maybe I should send up, like, a distress signal."

"There *were* flares on board," Jarek said mildly.

Jamal sniffed. "Flares are for wusses."

Tess laughed.

Even the police chief smiled.

And Faye hugged him tight.

Jamal hugged her back. Under his blackened jersey and bravado, his thin, lean frame was shaking.

"Anyway, it worked, didn't it?" he muttered against the top of her head.

Faye stepped back and smiled at him with tears in her eyes. "It sure did," she told him. "Thank you."

"It certainly speeded up response times for the rest of my department," Jarek said.

"And the fire department," Tess put in. "And the EMS crews."

The teenager sobered. "How's he doing? Denko. Aleksy, I mean."

"He should be in a room by now," Jarek said. He spoke to Jamal, but his attention was on Faye. "Would you like to see him?"

Her heart stuttered. "Can we?"

"Well, it's after visiting hours, but given that he was threatening to check himself out of here against medical advice if he didn't see you, I think the nurses will make an exception."

The nurse on the floor, a pretty, round-faced woman whose name tag identified her as Sherry Biddleman, was willing to make an exception about the hours. On the number of visitors, however, she held firm.

"Two at a time," she said. "I can't have a party in there waking the other patients."

"You two go," Tess said, giving Faye a nudge and Jamal a push. "I'll stay here and catch up with Sherry."

Faye hesitated. She wasn't family. "You're his brother…" she said to Jarek.

"And he's asking for you." He smiled reassurance. "Go."

Aleksy's eyes were closed when she entered his room. They had cut off his clothes and a lot of his hair. Above the bleached-out hospital gown, his face was gray with pain and dark with stubble. A line of black stitches marched across his strip-shaved scalp and puckered the arch of his forehead.

Faye's throat ached.

"Man, you look terrible," Jamal said.

The dark eyes opened, jolting her heartbeat.

"You're no prize either, kid," Aleksy said.

Jamal hunched a shoulder and approached the bed. "Huh. At least I don't look like Frankenstein."

"Nah. More like the Mummy."

Jamal grinned and touched the bandage wrapped around his head. "Like my new do-rag?"

"Yeah. It suits you." Seriously, Aleksy added, "You did good, Jamal."

Under his coffee-dark skin, the boy's color deepened. "Thanks, man. You, too."

They performed some complicated male hand ritual over the rails of the hospital bed that tired Faye just to watch. When they were done, Aleksy's hand slid limply onto the mattress.

She almost could not bear to see him so hurt, to see his vitality sapped by loss of blood and the drugs that ran into him through a tube in his vein.

She could not hide her feelings from herself any longer. She loved him.

And she was panicked, scared of the daily danger he faced and terrified his job would take him away from her.

It wasn't just the hospital bed and the blinking, bleeping machines she feared. Because she could accept that. If she loved him, if he admitted her even a little way into his life, then she had to accept that this might be only the first of many times she would stand in the door of a hospital room and see him lying there.

But if he loved her...oh, then it would be worth it. If he loved her, she could deal with the danger. She could put up with the hours and the absences and his preoccupation with the job. If he loved her.

He's not going to change, Tess had warned her.

He looked so pale.

She cleared her heart from her throat. "We should go. You need your rest."

"You're not leaving me," Aleksy protested.

And as simply as that, her decision was made.

She would not leave him. This time, she would not run away.

As long as it lasted, as long as he wanted her, she would stay.

Unable to resist any longer, she came to stand beside his bed. She wanted to touch him, needed the reassurance of his flesh. Constrained by Jamal's presence, frustrated by the lack of time, she stroked the back of Aleksy's hand. When he turned his palm over and laced his fingers with hers, she nearly wept.

"I should leave," she said. "Visiting hours are over."

He tightened his grip. "Stupid hospital rules."

With her free hand, she touched his rough jaw and the soft skin of his upper cheek.

"The rules are there to protect you," she scolded.

He smiled at her sleepily. "You sound like a cop."

No. She'd just lost her heart to one.

"When do you get out of here?" Jamal asked.

"They want to keep me for forty-eight hours' observation," Aleksy said. He looked back at Faye, his pupils black with drugs or promise. "I'll be out in twenty-four."

But it was thirty-six hours before the doctors released him.

Faye spent many of them at the hospital, but it seemed there was always someone else in Aleksy's room. Eric and Mary Denko came up from Chicago. Ten-year-old Allie spent half an hour one afternoon playing cards with her uncle on his hospital tray. Faye appreciated the loving support the Denkos gave one another, but it was hard not to feel excluded from that magic circle.

There was another brotherhood that made frequent

visits to Aleksy's hospital room. Faye thought of them as the league of men in suits. ATF. FBI. CTC. RCMP. She lost track of the initials. She had trouble telling them apart, these quiet-voiced men with their short haircuts and hard or tired eyes.

Defenders of our freedom, she told herself, and tried not to resent that they were keeping her from Aleksy. Tried not to mind when they came to her cottage with their tape recorders and persistent questions. Always in twos, like Noah's animal pairs, a race of navy gabardine, a breed apart.

This was what it was to love a cop.

This is what it meant to be involved in his case. In his life.

Outside of Aleksy's hospital room, Jarek tried to reassure her. "They're almost done. We picked up Freer and Amir the other night. The feds are happy. We can hold our suspects on charges of assault and attempted murder while they make their case on gunrunning and terrorism." Rare approval lit his eyes. "You were a big help."

"My bra in the cause of freedom," she said.

It didn't seem like enough.

It wasn't.

She had to repeat her story over and over to all the men and the one woman agent who came to question her. She signed statements and receipts for her broken camera and her photographs, and she waited for Aleksy to come back. To come home.

But would he?

With the men responsible for his partner's death finally locked up, what reason did he have to stay?

Her sense of isolation increased the following morning when Jamal announced his intention of returning to Chicago.

Faye, bleary from lack of sleep and the pain of her wrist, blinked at him. "But…your parents?"

"Hey, right now, I'm a hero. Denko called and told them all kinds of stories. I can do no wrong, you know?"

It had to be said.

"Jamal, you are going back to a place where it is far too easy to 'do wrong.'"

"Yeah. So?"

She held his gaze, willing him to take her seriously. "So, what are you going to do about that?"

"I'm clean now," he offered.

"That's a start. That's a good start. But you need to talk to someone who can help you stay clean."

"You mean, like a shrink?"

"Yes, or—"

"The county programs all got waiting lists. And my parents can't afford a private doc."

She was afraid he was right. "What about something like AA?"

"I was a druggie, Harp. Not a drunk. Anyway, that's for old people."

"It's for people who need help," she said.

"I don't need it. I messed up, but I'm okay now."

"Promise me you'll give it a shot anyway."

"Why?"

"Art lessons?" she suggested, and was rewarded when he shook his head with exasperated affection.

"You don't give up, do you?"

Not anymore.

It felt good.

She felt good.

"Nope," she said cheerfully. "How about you?"

"I guess I can't," he said. "Not if you're riding my ass all the time."

They grinned at each other.

Faye took a deep breath. "Now, about next year—"

"You're going to set up the meeting, right? With the guidance counselor and everybody?"

"Yes."

"Okay. So, I'll do the senior year thing for now. And then it's like you said. A bunch of colleges have fine arts programs. I'll apply to some schools and see what happens. It's not like I have to spend four years as a math major."

The hope in his voice moved her almost to tears. "You sound like you have this all figured out."

He shot her another smile. "Hey, I'm a genius. It's amazing how my mind works when I'm not tripping."

She laughed. And after he had packed, because it was what he wanted, she drove him to the train station.

"Take care of yourself," she told him seriously as they stood below the platform. "Call me anytime."

"I will," he promised. He hitched his book bag on his shoulder. "See you in September."

"In September," she echoed, and hugged him, and watched him climb the wooden steps away.

She went back to her empty cottage.

Standing in the middle of her temporary studio, she turned slowly in a circle, studying the flat, serene landscapes pinned to the wall and the one startling sunset still spread out on her worktable.

The bandage on her wrist was much less constrictive than her cast had been. Despite twinges when she flexed her arm, she could still paint.

Faye bit her lip. That is, she could if she had anything

to paint from. Her photos had been catalogued, confiscated or filed away. Her sketchbook, with its painting of the blown-up cabin cruiser, had been taken as evidence.

With all her prompts and aids gone, what did she have to work with?

She stared out the sliding glass doors at the lake. The remains of Richard Freer's dock stood up like black and broken teeth from the far shore, but the sky curved high and blue, and the lake glittered with promise.

Faye stood, irresolute, in her aunt Eileen's living room. A freshening breeze slipped through the window to tease her hair and toy with the edges of the paper on the table.

Suddenly, she moved. She collected her paints and her palette, her brushes and a mayonnaise jar filled with water, and carried them all outside. She lugged her easel outside, too, bumping it down the wooden steps, and set it up on the dry grass.

The bright scene before her beckoned. Picking up her brush, Faye dipped it in the water and began to paint.

From the heart.

From life.

That was how Aleksy found her an hour later, standing outside in her bare feet and long skirt, her hair golden in the sunlight. Paint tubes spotted the grass around her like flowers.

The utter rightness of the scene soothed his restless spirit, so that for long moments he was content simply to watch her.

But what he had come to say jumped and burned inside him like water drops on a hot griddle.

His throat worked. "Faye."

Just her name, but it was enough to make her turn and look at him.

And the welcome in her eyes nearly stopped his heart.

"Aleksy! You're home."

She dropped her brush and ran across the grass toward him. It was great. Beyond great. It was everything he'd ever wanted and hadn't known he was searching for.

He kissed her. Her lips warmed under his and clung. She was sweeter than summer wine, more addictive than any drug. Her body pressed, slim and firm, against his. Her bare toes climbed his shoes. For a minute, he forgot what he had to say.

"Faye." He broke the kiss. And then, because her mouth was so hot and so close, had to kiss her again. "Faye."

Those pink lips curved. "You said that already."

"Yeah."

God, he had to have her. Now would be best, but soon would have to do. They had to talk.

"We have to talk," he said.

She stiffened a little in his arms. "Now?"

He was pretty sure it had to be now. Otherwise, she'd have his tongue tangled and his mind completely blown, and it might be hours before he got back to the subject at hand, so to speak.

"Yeah," he said again.

She didn't look so thrilled about that. He understood. He was anxious to get on to the next part himself. But he thought—hoped—she'd be happier after she heard him out.

"The thing is—" He lost himself a moment in her big chocolate brown eyes, in the feel of her, warm and sweetly curved against him. What was the thing again? "We can't go on like this," he said.

Her arms slid from around his neck. "No?"

"No." He almost raked a hand through his hair; remembered the bullet graze and stuck both hands in his pockets instead. Jeez, he was nervous. Embarrassed, he tried to make a joke of it. "The thing is, now that they've met you, my parents practically expect us to get married. Allie wants to be a bridesmaid."

Faye's face whitened. "I'm sorry if our—involvement—has created a problem with your family."

Where was her sense of humor? "Yes. No. The thing is—"

She raised her hand. "Before you go any further, may I say something, please?"

Frustrated, he glared at her. Maybe she should. He certainly wasn't getting anywhere on his own.

"Go ahead," he invited.

She took a deep breath. "I just want you to know that I don't intend to make this difficult for you. You can leave at any time."

Aleksy felt like he'd taken another bullet. In the heart, this time.

First the shock. *Numbing, cold.*

And then the pain. *Searing, hot.*

"You just can't forgive me, can you?" he asked bitterly.

"Forgive you for what?"

But he'd heard the accusation too many times before to believe he wasn't already charged, tried, and convicted.

"For thinking like a cop. Reacting like a cop, instead of your lover."

Her brow pleated. "No, I just told you—"

But he rolled over her, desperate to explain. Practically begging her to understand, for God's sake. "I know I promised to take care of you. But if I'd given myself up the other night, the way Freer wanted, it wouldn't have saved you."

"I know that."

"I had to wait for a clear shot."

"Aleksy, I know that."

"He would have killed us both otherwise."

Her eyes snapped. "I'm not stupid. You don't have to explain to me that if you hadn't responded to the situation according to your training, if you hadn't—what did you say?—reacted like a cop, we'd both be dead right now."

"Then—then why do you want me to leave?"

"I don't." Her face softened. Her voice gentled. "Aleksy, I don't love you in spite of what you do. I love you because of who you are. And part of who you are is your job."

Despite the fact that she was talking to him as if he were one of her students, he was having trouble understanding her.

Maybe it was the fracture in his skull.

Or maybe it was the pounding of his heart.

"You love me?" he repeated carefully.

She frowned. "Of course I do."

He gave up. She loved him. "Then why are we arguing?"

"I don't know." Her lips curved. "Because you haven't tried anything else?"

Right. He might have a bullet graze in his head, but he wasn't too stupid to recognize an invitation when he heard one. He reached for her.

Faye went into his arms with a shudder of relief. He was alive. He was here. And he was hers.

For now.

They kissed gently, a hello-how-are-you kind of kiss, exploring, tender. And his lips were so soft and his mouth was so hot and he felt so good, warm and solid against her, that she forgot about his wound and kissed him again, harder this time.

She felt his chest expand as he inhaled sharply and kissed her back, wrapping her tightly against him. His chest was hard. His arms were hard. His shoulders were rigid with control. Faye smiled against his mouth. He was hard all over.

She ran her hands down his back while they kissed. She was drowning in his kisses, deeper now, devouring, while the sun poured over them like honey, warm, sticky, sweet. Her limbs were loosening, her insides softening, her mind melting under the force of the sun, under the heat of his kiss.

His mouth was urgent on the point of her chin, the side of her neck, the hollow of her throat. His beard prickled her skin. The warm grass prickled her feet. She sucked in her breath. His hot hands covered her breasts. His thumbs rubbed her nipples. She moaned. She wanted more. More heat. More sensation. More Aleksy.

She slid her hands under his shirt, greedy for the feel of his flesh, warm and smooth and muscled beneath her fingers.

"Let's move this inside," he said, his voice rough.

She opened her eyes. "No."

His thumbs stilled. "No?"

"I want you now," she said, hot and embarrassed. But it was true. "Outside. In the sun. No hiding."

"Here," he said, looking as if he couldn't believe her.

"Yes."

"Outside."

She burned. "Yes."

"Kind of kinky for a schoolteacher," he said, but he didn't sound disapproving. He sounded amused. Excited.

Willing.

"Please," she said.

"I told you before, you could have anything if you begged," he said hoarsely, and proceeded to give her…everything.

He laid her on the bank and covered her, his body lean and hard against her front while the soft grass tickled her back and legs. He pulled her shirt up and over her head. His mouth was wet and seeking against her breasts. His hands tugged at her skirt and glided, warm and rough, against her sensitized flesh. He filled her with his fingers and she gasped, her bare feet planted against the earth, the sun burning her eyelids, his kiss burning her mouth, his touch searing between her legs.

And then he stopped. A cool breeze ran over her thighs and stomach.

"Aleksy!"

"Shh," he said, laughter shaking his voice. "You're scaring the ducks."

"Screw the ducks," she said.

He laughed, and then his gaze, hot and intent, narrowed and focused on her face. "I can think of better things to do."

She shivered with love and lust and need. *Yes.*

He reached for his pants and covered himself with a condom. She lifted her hips and then—oh, yes—he was thick and hot at her body's entrance. He was there, inside her.

She screamed and clawed at him. He bit her mouth, licked her lip, pushed his way inside her, over and over, again and again, coming into her, coming.

She shattered around him and he thrust into her, tensed against her, his breath hot on her face. And then his hands tightened on her. He groaned into her hair and was still.

Faye thought maybe he was dead.

Maybe they both were and this was heaven.

Paradise, she thought, drifting. Eden. She felt warm and relaxed. Mated. Created only for this one man for the rest of their lives together.

"Like Adam and Eve," she murmured.

Aleksy stirred. "What?"

He would run a million miles away if she told him what she was thinking.

She smiled at him ruefully. "It's not important."

He frowned. His body was damp and heavy against hers. "Faye—"

Oh, dear. She could feel the tension returning to his muscles. She stroked the side of his face.

"Don't worry about it," she said, soothing, tender. "I won't ask for more than you're prepared to give."

Like all your other women, she thought, but did not say. She had given him her heart. Let her keep her pride.

He rolled off of her. "Well, that's a crock."

She sat up. "Excuse me?"

His jaw set. "I told you, you don't expect enough of me."

"You told me a lot of things." She reached for her shirt, covered her breasts, feeling suddenly exposed and vulnerable. "Including that there is no happily ever after."

He swore. "I knew we should talk first." He glared at her. "But you distracted me."

Faye raised her chin. She was not going to run. She was not going to hide. She was not going to apologize for her feelings. "I told you I loved you."

He was digging in the pants pocket that had held the condom. "That's what I meant. How am I supposed to think when you say stuff like that?"

She couldn't think, either. "I don't expect—"

"Got it." He threw away the pants and rolled to his knees. He took her hand.

And there, on the green and yellow grass, with dragonflies mating in spectacular flight and a family of mallards setting up house beside the water, Aleksy Denko got down on both knees before her.

"Okay, listen up," he said. "Because I've never done the asking before and I'll probably botch it up, so you need to pay attention."

She started to tremble. "Pay attention to what?"

He frowned. "I think you should be standing."

She was bewildered. Fascinated. "You want me to stand?"

"I just said so, didn't I?" he snapped, and then shook his head. "God. I'm botching this already. I'm no good at talking. I should have asked you straight out to begin with."

"Asked me what?"

"To marry me." He looked up, and the certainty in his eyes stilled her nerves and rattled her heart. A great, warm flood of joy rose from her toes and washed through her. "I know it's a lot, asking you to take on the life of a cop's wife, but—"

He fumbled with the box in his hand—a dark blue velvet jeweler's box. She stared, shaking, as he opened it, revealing a sparkling diamond solitaire set in a swoop of gold.

More than he could afford, she was sure.

And far, far more than she expected.

His gaze was very steady. His hands were not. "I love you," he said. "And I'm asking for all your love and the rest of our lives. Will you? Will you marry me, Faye?"

Her breath caught. Her eyes filled. She held out her hand and watched as he slid the ring with its heart of fire onto her finger. Its colors flashed and glowed in the sunlight.

Her future stretched before her—a perfect canvas she could fill with color and life and love.

"With all my heart," she said, and leaned forward, and kissed him.

*   *   *   *   *

There's still more TROUBLE IN EDEN *ahead.*
Look for Mark's secret past to come out in
ALL A MAN CAN BE this April!

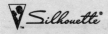